There's

# Gotta be

# Something More

There's

# Gotta be
## Something More

## Maggie Grey

Black Lyon Publishing, LLC

**THERE'S GOTTA BE SOMETHING MORE**
Copyright © 2009 by MARIA COLEY

Our books may be ordered through your local bookstore or by visiting the publisher:

**www.BlackLyonPublishing.com**

Black Lyon Publishing, LLC
PO Box 567
Baker City, OR 97814

This is a work of fiction. All of the characters, names, events, organizations and conversations in this novel are either the products of the author's vivid imagination or are used in a fictitious way for the purposes of this story.

ISBN-10:      1-934912-12-3
ISBN-13:    978-1-934912-12-6
Library of Congress Control Number:   2008939188

Written, published and printed in
the United States of America.

**Black Lyon Contemporary Romance**

*To my husband and daughter—*
*my pride, my joy, my love.*

# Chapter One

When she stepped through the front door, a feeling of coming home after a long trip swept through her. Her eyes scanned the interior of the house; it was exactly what she was looking for. The living area was one large room. The log walls and vaulted ceilings made the room spacious and gave it a rustic look. There was an oversized stone fireplace to the left. Directly ahead were stairs leading to the second floor. The kitchen and dining area were to the right.

But what made this home so spectacular were the windows that made up the right wall. They ran from floor to ceiling and looked out onto the most beautiful scenery Jesse had ever seen.

Outside the windows was a deck that ran the length of the house. Jesse stepped outside, closed her eyes and took a deep breath. She could smell the wildflowers that grew in the fields beyond, hear birds and water flowing in the distance.

About fifty yards from the house sat a weather-worn barn with pastures behind it. Beyond that, the land was untouched. Lush vegetation covered gently rolling hills leading to mountains that formed a horseshoe around the land, protecting it from the outside. There were two-hundred-seventy-five acres total, more than enough for what she wanted to do.

"I'll take it," she said.

The realtor smiled in approval.

Jesse walked with him back to the car. They had been driving around Montana for a week looking at different ranches. Jesse knew what she was looking for. She had pictured it enough times in her mind, and when she stepped out of the car today, her dreams had come to life.

Moving from Connecticut to Montana was a huge step—one she'd thought about often over the past two years. At almost forty, Jesse had known her life was not what she wanted it to be. Now, newly divorced from a man she'd been with for almost twenty years, Jesse wanted her life to be just that—*her* life.

When she first met Paul, he was an aspiring rock star, a lead singer who was good looking and reckless. Why this had appealed to her, Jesse couldn't remember. All the guys wanted to be his friend and all the girls just wanted him, but he had chosen her. Not that she was bad looking.

Jesse always felt she was a little overweight, but that's what you get for having friends who were always thin without trying. Her Italian heritage just didn't allow for that. Some would call her voluptuous, but at five four, Jesse just always felt fat. Brown hair and eyes, nothing special about them, but skin that had few wrinkles made Jesse look years younger. She'd worked hard to drop the thirty pounds that had been hanging around for the past few years, and felt fantastic.

As they drove away from the ranch, Jesse asked how soon they could close on the property.

"That will depend on how quickly the mortgage company can get the paperwork together. But since the place is empty—"

"We don't need a mortgage company," Jesse cut in. "I'm paying cash."

Ken glanced at her. He had never asked if she would be able to afford the mortgage on a place like this. Although small, it was still eight-hundred-thousand dollars.

"Cash?" he asked.

"Yes. I can have the funds transferred as soon as the papers are ready," she said, smiling.

A cash sale was unusual, but the quicker the closing, the

less likely a buyer would back out.

"Okay, I'll see what I can do."

With that settled, Jesse asked, "Do you know of a hotel in this area I can stay at? I'd like to start exploring, and look into contractors to build a new barn."

"There's an inn that would probably work. It's family-run and clean."

Anything clean and safe would work. Jesse didn't plan on doing much there but sleep.

She only had four more weeks to move in and get settled before she had to pick up her daughter. Emma was spending a month with Jesse's parents. Once school started, Jesse wasn't sure when they would be able to visit. She was going to be very busy trying to get a business off the ground in a town where no one knew her.

Jesse had chosen Montana for two reasons. She wanted a home with land, but not just any land. The land had to be full of life, and there had to be mountains. She could already picture herself sitting on the deck with her morning coffee looking out at those mountains.

The second reason was a bit silly, but ever since she'd seen *Legends of the Fall* with Brad Pitt, she'd wanted to come to Montana.

As she watched the scenery go by, Jesse thought about the incredible luck that made it possible for her to be here.

Everyday she had gone to work and when she got paid, so did the bills. The credit card debt that was holding her back finally started to go down. She couldn't even remember what had been bought, but she knew if the debt was gone, she could leave Paul.

It was horrible to think she stayed with him because of financial reasons. He said he loved her. She just didn't love him. They had grown apart and her feelings for him had changed. She couldn't stay in a marriage where she was unhappy. He deserved more—they both did. A big house, nice car and clothes, they just weren't what she really wanted. She realized that these things weren't as important as being happy with herself.

She finally got it after she started helping a friend who worked with children with disabilities. Volunteering made Jesse feel like she was finally doing something for someone else, and it felt really good. Seeing these children made Jesse realize how truly lucky she was, and how much she took for granted.

She wanted to instill good morals in Emma, who was becoming spoiled. Jesse cut back on buying things, and when she did buy something, she questioned if she really needed whatever it was. She also quit buying things for Emma whenever they were out. Emma started to have chores and get an allowance to buy what she wanted.

Emma was one of the reasons Jesse wanted to make a life change. The other was a horse named Bear.

Bear came into Jesse's life unexpectedly. A seventeen-hand grey quarter horse with a personality any owner would kill for. When a friend approached Jesse about buying Bear and putting some training into him to resell, it had seemed like a way to make a quick bit of money.

"It would only be for a few months," she'd said. "He's a great horse with a lot of potential. We should be able to sell him before the show season is over."

Sounded like a plan. A few thousand dollars in, and they could double the investment in a few months. Jesse saw the debt going down as they planned Bear's training. Eight months later, Bear was still in training, and Jesse loved him more than ever. Whatever possessed her to think she would want to give this horse up? Jesse became emotionally attached to every animal she had ever owned, and some she didn't.

Bear turned out to be a great learner. He was willing and eager and had not one mean bone in his body. A leg injury made training slow and the show season ended. Working all winter to have him ready for the next season was the new plan. Spring arrived and Bear was ready. Pictures and descriptions were posted on all horse web sites, flyers sent to local barns. But it seemed like no one wanted this great horse.

People came to look.

"Does he do flying changes?"

"We're working on those," Jesse would answer.

"Can he jump three foot?" they'd ask.

"Um, he's up to two six right now."

Jesse's heart broke at the thought of selling Bear. This horse had become hers. He trusted her and she him. The thought of losing Bear set Jesse on a path to gaining financial stability. But that stability did not come soon enough and Bear was sold.

*He was going to a good home, but not as good of a home as I would have given him,* Jesse thought. Jesse vowed never again to have to give up something she loved due to financial reasons.

Then one day everything changed. After fighting with Paul over money before she left for work, Jesse stopped for gas. Feeling more down than ever, she fished her last dollar out of her purse after she saw the guy in front of her buy a lottery ticket for that night's drawing. She had never been lucky, but thought, *What the hell, life couldn't get much worse.*

The next morning Jesse's heart stopped when she looked at the winning numbers on her computer screen and realized they were the same on her tickets. Staring open-mouthed was all she could do. Two-hundred and fifty-million dollars was the jackpot and one winning ticket. Her winning ticket. Was she dreaming? This couldn't be real. Should she get up and leave? Finish the day at work? Scream and tell everyone?

Jesse smiled to herself as she remembered that day. She finished working, or at least being at work. How can you actually work knowing you no longer had to? When she got home she started making plans because all her dreams were about to become a reality.

# Chapter Two

*J*esse was up and dressed early the next day. She flipped through the phone book and made calls to potential contractors. Two were available to meet with her later that day.

Hungry, she decided to try the diner she'd seen the night before. *No time like the present to start meeting the townspeople,* she thought.

Hickory Diner was like most small diners. The white walls and blue chairs gave it a bright, friendly look. Jesse was surprised at how crowded the diner was. Of the ten stools at the bar, at least half were taken. Each of the tables had at least three people at them. The booths were all full, but Jesse noticed a couple getting up and sat down when they moved away.

Jesse could see covered plates on the counter that held muffins and cakes, and hear the sizzle of the grill. Smelling the bacon cooking made her stomach growl.

"Coffee?" a waitress asked as she cleared away the cups that had been left.

"Yes, and a western omelet, please."

The waitress looked to be in her early twenties, tall, maybe five seven, with blond hair pulled into a ponytail. She had beautiful almond shaped hazel eyes and full lips that Jesse would kill for.

When the waitress left, Jesse opened the paper she had picked up on the way in. Once she had the barn ready, she wanted to get a few horses. Looking through the classifieds, she saw several possibilities.

"What are you looking for?" the waitress asked as she set the coffee mug down. "I've lived here all my life and can probably tell you where to go."

"I'm buying the vacant ranch out off Route 15 and I wanted start looking around for some horses for when the barn is ready," Jesse replied.

"Best place around here to get good horses is out at the Triple S. If they don't have what you want, Zach can usually find it for you."

"Thanks, I'll keep that in mind." *No time like the present to start making friends*, Jesse thought as she held out her hand and smiled. "I'm Jesse."

"Jen McKinnon. Your friendly Hickory Diner waitress," she replied, shaking Jesse's hand.

"Nice to meet you, Jen."

"Just give me a holler if you need anything else," Jen said as she turned to walk away.

Jesse finished her breakfast, left a generous tip and waved to Jen on her way out.

•

Having an hour before her first contractor appointment, Jesse wondered the streets of Dillon. Before coming to Montana she'd done some research and decided that the southwestern corner of the state would be best for her. The weather was in the 80s in the summer and although cold in the winter, the area got less snow than the rest of the state. Butte, Helena, and Bozeman were all within driving distance if Jesse felt the need to go to a larger city.

Dillon was a perfect sized town. The older parts of it reminded Jesse of the town of Mayberry on the *Andy Griffith Show*. The buildings had a historical ambiance to them. The storefronts had colorful awnings and signs. The windows were decorated with items that each store held.

As she walked down Main Street, Jesse saw signs pointing out the direction of a hospital, schools, theater and college. There was a park in the center of town, and Jesse could see children playing. A statue of the town's founder stood in the center.

Continuing on, Jesse came across what she thought would become one of her most frequented stores, Baker Tack & Feed. A bell jingled as Jesse opened the door. Stepping in she realized the store was much larger than it looked from the outside.

Besides the feed section, which was at the back of the store, there was a section with a wide variety of western tack and blankets, a general horse care section with brushes, shampoos, supplements and such. But by far the largest section by far was the clothing section.

Rows of cowboy boots and jeans, along with racks of colorful cowboy shirts for men and women took up a good third of the store. *Guess I'll have to buy my English riding clothes on the internet.*

Although she had ridden western for pleasure when she was younger, her riding career consisted mostly of English saddles, breeches and boots. Jesse had no problem with riding western, but she didn't want to totally abandon her English ways. She also knew there was more to riding western than just sitting in the saddle, so that meant lessons.

"Can I help you find something?"

Blue eyes surrounded by a weathered face and a welcoming smile greeted Jesse when she turned around. The man wore a blue and white checkered shirt with a black leather vest on top, wrangler jeans, and worn cowboy boots.

Jesse had just come face to face with her first real cowboy. So what if he was old enough to be her grandfather. He definitely had the cowboy look down, bowed legs and all.

Jesse smiled brightly. "No, just taking a look around."

"Passing through town?" the man asked.

"Actually no," she answered. "I'm buying the vacant ranch out off Route 15. I'm Jesse."

"Bill Baker," he said, taking the hand she offered.

"Baker? Are you the owner?"

"For forty-three years now. Whatever you need we have

and if not, we can get it for you," Bill said proudly.

"I'll keep that in mind for when I get some horses."

"Horses huh? Don't have any yet?" he asked.

Jesse shook her head.

"Well, you'll want to go out to the Triple S."

"Jen over at the diner mentioned the Triple S. Are you talking about the same one?" Jesse asked.

"The same. Zach's my grandson. But I'm not telling you he has the best horses around because of that. He's got the touch of knowing a good horse from a rotten one. Only deals in the best."

"Maybe you could good give me some directions after you give me a tour of your wonderful store." At the small compliment Bill gave her a smile that touched his eyes.

Bill took the time to show her around, only stopping briefly to greet customers as they came in the door. He greeted everyone by name and always asked how the family was. He also introduced her to everyone, not that she would remember many names. After spending a good forty-five minutes, Jesse told Bill she had to go. Her meeting with the contractor was in fifteen minutes.

"What do you need contractors for?" Bill inquired.

"The barn that's there needs some repairs and I'd also like to build a larger barn with an indoor ring," she replied.

"Really, what do you need with all that space?" Bill asked.

"I want to start a therapeutic riding school and will need the larger barn for school horses, as well as for boarders. The indoor ring will be needed during bad weather and in the winter."

Bill smiled at her answer. "Be sure to ask Zach about contractors when you see him. He'll let you know who you can trust and who you can't."

"I'll do that. I appreciate you taking the time to personally show me around. I'll be back when I'm ready to outfit the new barn."

"Make sure you do. For now though you may want to

come back and pick up some real boots," Bill said, eyeing Jesse's sneakers. His smile reached his eyes when he said it. Jesse knew he was a man who had charmed the ladies in his younger days.

Assuring Bill she would be back, Jesse left for her meeting with the contractor.

# Chapter Three

After meeting with the contractors she'd found, Jesse drove out Route 15 to the Triple S. The meetings had gone well and both contractors seemed to know what they were doing. She knew the barn addition and indoor ring would be expensive, so she wasn't surprised at the preliminary estimates. Talking with the contractors made Jesse realize she would need some help. The project was going to be big and her knowledge of building barns was minimal.

Looking down at the directions Bill had given her to the Triple S, Jesse realized the turn-off was the same as the ranch she was buying. Bill had mentioned that the Triple S was just past hers, but she didn't think it was on the same road.

Jesse felt a sense of pride as she drove by the long driveway leading up to her ranch. *My ranch*, she thought. *I'll need a name.* Something fun, something that fit her new life. High Hopes Riding. A New Start Equestrian.

Although it was almost four miles from her driveway to the Triple S, there were no other ranches in between, which meant Zach Baker was her neighbor. *Is he still a neighbor if he's four miles away?* In Montana that would be a yes.

Going under the sign for the Triple S, Jesse could see a gray ranch style house with a wraparound front porch off to the left. To the right were pastures. The barns and corral were straight past the house. And behind it all were those beautiful mountains. The view at the Triple S was almost as good as the view from her new place. Almost.

Jesse parked near the other vehicles in front of the barn. Not seeing anyone, she got out and walked toward the corral where there was a beautiful brown and white horse standing looking at the newcomer.

"Well hello there, gorgeous," Jesse said as she scratched the horse's muzzle.

"Why thank you. No one's called me gorgeous in a long time."

Startled, Jesse looked toward the barn to see a short, stocky man walking toward her. He wore a similar outfit to Bill Baker, except his clothes were worn from working outside. The only thing he had that Bill didn't was a well-worn cowboy hat. Two cowboys in one day; Jesse knew she was in the West.

"I'm looking for Zach Baker. When I told Bill at the feed store I was looking to buy some horses he told me Zach was the one to see," Jesse said cheerfully.

"Bill, huh?" He seemed to size Jesse up. "Zach's out back," he said and turned back toward the barn.

Since Jesse was not sure where "out back" was, she followed him. "Great ranch," she said.

"Sure is."

*Talkative fellow.* As they walked through the barn, Jesse noticed about twelve regular stalls and a few double stalls. She assumed the double was a birthing stall, which meant the Triple S did some breeding. The barn was neat and well kept, and smelled of fresh hay and horses. Jesse approved. A neat barn usually meant well-cared-for horses.

Stepping out the backside of the barn Jesse saw more pastures, a round pen, and riding ring.

"Zach! You have a visitor."

Jesse's attention was drawn to a group of men fencing the far left pasture. The two facing her looked up, and Jesse noticed they were twins. Young, maybe early twenties, built, blond and gorgeous. *Hello.*

When the man with his back to her finally turned, Jesse hoped her jaw didn't hit the ground too hard. The man had to be at least six two with broad shoulders, correction, broad sweaty shoulders attached to a chest that tapered down to defined abs, all of which was fitted into jeans that sat low enough to show the top of his hip bones, and promised to be holding a piece heaven in them.

Jesse sighed as he walked over to where she was standing. Zach Baker was Jesse's cowboy fantasy come to life.

"This is—" the man paused and looked over at Jesse in question.

"Jesse," she said trying not to let the drool drip out of her mouth.

"Bill sent her out here to see you about some horses."

"Thanks, Bob," Zach said turning his attention to her.

Jesse caught her breath. He was even better up close. The man had the most beautiful blue eyes she had ever seen. They reminded her of a new unwashed pair of jeans. He had at least a day's beard on his face and his skin was tanned from working outside. His face was rugged but very handsome. His light brown hair was tussled and Jesse felt an urge to reach out and push the pieces that had fallen toward his eyes away.

"Nice to meet you," Jesse said, holding out her hand. Zach looked her over as he pulled off the leather work gloves he was wearing.

This man oozed sexuality, and when his hand took hers, Jesse felt a warm sensation ripple through her.

"Pleasure," he said, keeping eye contact with her.

"Your ranch is beautiful," she said, withdrawing her hand. "Do you do your own breeding?"

Zach had started to walk toward the barn so Jesse followed. He walked into what looked like an office and came out with a drink.

"Some. I have one mare who will foal in a few weeks. But usually I use other breeders and work more as a middleman. If I find a horse I like, I'll keep it here and do some training until I feel it's ready to sell," he answered her as he sat on a hay bale. Then taking a drink he asked, "What kind of horses are you looking for?"

"Well, I uh—" Jesse watched as he used the back of his arm to wipe the sweat from his forehead. She tried not to stare at the way his ab muscles tightened whenever he moved. "I'm not really sure," she said. Actually she knew exactly what she was looking for, it's just she was a little distracted right now. She really wished he'd put a shirt on.

Zach looked at her with those gorgeous eyes and she thought she would melt into the ground. Walking over to stand by a stall, she reached out to pet the horse in it. She knew he was judging her. She could tell by the bored look on his face that he thought she was a joke.

•

When Jesse turned to the horse she was petting, Zach allowed his gaze to travel over her. He'd known she was coming. His grandfather had already called to tell him she was on her way. Zach knew she was new in town, and buying the ranch next to his.

"Be nice. She's a city girl," Bill had said, making it sound as if he wouldn't be. Zach had already formed an impression of her before she even got here.

She probably didn't know one horse from another. He did, however, have to admit she was very attractive. Dressed in a plain white T-shirt and a worn pair of jeans that fell low enough on her waist if she moved just right he could see the skin of her stomach. *Nice*, he thought taking a drink, *very nice*.

Her brown hair was just past her shoulders and held back from her face by sunglasses. Her eyes were the color of melted chocolate. She had an amazing hourglass shape, and when Zach had shook her hand, he felt an instant sexual attraction.

Taking a deep, impatient breath, he decided she needed more help than she let on. "Let's start this way then. What do you plan to do with them?" he asked slowly and deliberately.

Jesse could hear the impatience in his voice. He'd asked her the question as if she were a child. She had always been uncomfortable around men. Attractive ones were even worse.

Her newfound confidence was slowly fading.

Feeling the anger building in her, Jesse turned to him with a brilliant smile pasted on her face, "I plan on opening a vacation dude ranch so people like me, you know, from the city, can come out for a western adventure. Cattle driving, roping, that kind of stuff. Money is no object," she said raising her chin in what she hoped was a snobbish manner.

Jesse couldn't help it, she saw the way he was looking at her, like some inexperienced, rich city girl who was out here just for kicks. The sarcastic tone in his voice had pissed her off.

Zach's drink stopped midway to his lips. The look on his face was a cross between shock and annoyance.

Jesse turned back toward the horse to keep from laughing.

"I know there are a lot of places like that near here, but I think I can make mine really special," she said as she turned to him again. "One idea I had was if I can find some good looking cowboys to work on the ranch I could have a girl's vacation package."

Jesse paused and looked directly at him, then began to pace in front of him, using her arms to try and add to the excitement she didn't feel.

"City women love to get away from it all, and what better place than here? It's so beautiful, romantic, secluded."

She dared a glance at him. Was he buying this crap?

"If I add a pool, some tennis courts and hired some great looking guys and dressed them in chaps, cowboy hats, and no shirts of course," she said, closing her eyes.

"Of course," Zach mumbled.

"Mm, I can see it now." Jesse opened her eyes and smiled broadly at him.

Walking over to where Zach was sitting, she stopped in front of him and let her eyes roll over him appreciatively.

"Maybe you'd be interested in a job?" Reaching out she ran a finger over his shoulder and down his bicep. "Save a horse ride a cowboy," she said smiling at him suggestively.

Zach's mouth dropped open. Holy crap! What was his grandfather thinking sending her out here? A girl's vacation package where good looking cowboys were the draw. He had heard some crazy ideas in his life, but this one took the cake.

Jesse watched him and tried to keep the anger she felt off her face. Did her really think she was serious? God help her, why was she still here? Looping her thumbs in the front pockets of her jeans she tried to look totally innocent as she waited for some reply.

"I can see you're in the middle of something." She looked toward the men still repairing the fence. "Would it be better if I, ah, came back another time? When there's no one else around."

Zach followed her gaze. He wasn't sure how to answer her. He didn't want her to come back at all.

Sure she was hot and his skin still burned from where she'd touched his shoulder, but there was no way in hell he was selling her horses for what she had in mind.

"I'm not sure I can help you," Zach said as he stood. "Trail horses really aren't my thing."

Jesse pouted out her lips and looked up at him. "Really? Everyone I talked to said you're the best person to get horses from. And I want the best for my ranch," she said as she looked down then back up at him through lowered eyelids. "I'd do anything to get you to help me," she said licking her lips as she took a step closer. *I'm going straight to hell for this,* she thought.

Zach watched her and felt his blood start to race. She might be crazy, but she was turning him on. Zach ran his hands through his hair. He was going to kill his grandfather.

"Fine. I'll see what I can find for you."

Jesse squealed and clapped her hands together like a girl who had just gotten her way. She knew she was only confirming what he already thought of her, but too bad.

"Really? This is going to be the best vacation ranch ever," she said. "I'm staying at the inn in town for now. You can reach me there."

Jesse smiled at him and turned to walk toward her car. As her smile turned to a scowl she rolled her eyes. *Jerk,* she thought.

Zach shook his head as he turned to go back to work. As soon as he finished with the fence he would call his grandfather and have him deal with her. He had gotten him into this and now he could get him out.

# Chapter Four

*J*esse finished the e-mail she was writing and hit "send." She was proud of herself for the way she handled Zach Baker today. Sure she had lied to him, but he deserved it. Let him think what he wanted to, she didn't want help from anyone who wouldn't give her a chance. He had formed an opinion of her before she'd even opened her mouth.

She was through with men who thought they were superior and had no interest in women other than for sex. If and when she decided to get involved with anyone she had a list of criteria he needed to meet. She had raised the bar on her standards and not even a hot body would make her give in.

She did have to admit, though, that Zach had one body she'd like to give in to.

Hearing a knock, and assuming her dinner had arrived, she opened the door to find the man himself standing there. "Mr. Baker," she said surprised. "What can I do for you?"

Jesse thought he was a jerk, but obviously her body had not heard. At seeing him, Jesse felt a tingle between her legs. His blue eyes looked down at her and Jesse felt as if he was burning her with them.

He looked amazing. She wanted to open the door and invite his jean-clad butt in for the night. He looked like he had showered, but his hair was uncombed and he hadn't shaven. Rugged and sexy—just the way the new Jesse liked her men.

Zach entered the room and closed the door, forcing her to take a step back. "You offered me a job. I've come to apply," he said, giving Jesse a grin that gave her goosebumps.

"What?" she said backing up as he walked past her.

"After you left I was thinking that it might be fun, ya know," he said with a shrug. "Working around women who basically worshipped your body. Of course I could only work part-time because of the ranch. Thought I might give it a try," he said as he walked over to stand by the bed.

His cocky smile made Jesse feel like she was way out of her league. This time it was Jesse's turn to gape open mouthed at him. Was he that stupid and full of himself to have believed her?

Zach walked over to Jesse, placing his hands on her shoulders then ran them down her arms.

His touch sent a shudder through her. "What, what are you doing?" she asked, her voice unsteady.

Cupping her face in his hands, Zach gave her a slow grin. "I figured this would be a hands-on interview."

Before she could protest Zach's lips touched hers and a hot sensation ran from Jesse's lips to her feet, then back up making her whole body feel like it was on fire.

She brought her hands between them with the intention of pushing him away, but instead settled them on his chest. The cotton of his shirt was soft and she could feel his rock hard, muscled chest underneath.

*I'll stop him in just a second,* she thought as she opened her mouth and let his tongue slide in.

•

After Jesse left the ranch, Zach finished the fence work, cleaned up and went to see his grandfather.

At first his grandfather sounded as nuts as she did. "So what do you think of her plans? Pretty ambitious don't you think? It could bring a lot of jobs to the area."

"Sure, if that's the kind of job you'd want," Zach grumbled.

"Why wouldn't you? If I were younger I'd probably apply. It sounds like it would be very fulfilling."

Zach stared at his grandfather. The job would be fulfilling

alright. Picking up a box from behind the counter he followed his grandfather to the storage room. "Why in the world would you think I would want to sell her horses?"

"She said she wanted the best horses. Needed them to be safe for the kids."

"Kids?" Why would there be kids at what sounded like an adult porn ranch?

"She seems really ambitious, that one. Working with disabled kids isn't easy."

Zach stopped. Disabled kids were a far cry from sexy cowboys and horny women. She had lied to him. One thing Zach despised was people who lied.

Not wanting his grandfather to see how angry he was he left the store and headed toward the hotel without thinking. He had every intention of teaching her a lesson, but when she had opened the door the raw desire that had hit him at the ranch did so again.

When she moaned, Zach decided it was time to end the kiss … in a minute. Her lips were so soft and she was more than willing to let him have his way with them. He slid his lips off hers, and she turned her head allowing him access to her neck.

Things weren't going exactly as Zach had planned. They were getting carried away. The kiss had affected him physically.

The minute he put his lips on hers, he'd started to get hard. From a kiss. What was up with that? He had more control over himself than to let a kiss get to him. He was supposed to be angry with her.

"So what do you think?" he asked, his voice husky. "Can I have the job?"

Jesse wasn't sure what to think. The kiss had her body aching to be touched. Zach's body was hard against her and she was sure she felt something through his jeans.

She needed to tell him the truth and make him leave. When she looked up into his eyes, then down at those lips that had just given her more pleasure than she'd felt in a very long time, she lost any sane thoughts.

"I think I might need to have you back for a second interview," she said as she put her arms around his neck and pulled him down to her.

He'd been in control of the first kiss, now she had taken control. Her kiss was hungry. Because she had her arms around him she was able to pull her body against his and he had wrapped his arms around her waist.

Jesse pressed her body against Zach loving the feeling of him. She attacked his mouth with a passion she never knew she had. Every ounce of her wanted this man. She wanted to feel him against her, on her, in her.

Zach broke away from her and stepped back. Looking at her, he took another step away. She was breathing heavily and her lips were swollen, her eyelids lowered. All he had to do was push her back onto the bed.

"Let's go," he said grabbing her hand he leading her to the door. He wasn't finished with her yet.

"Where are we going?"

Zach looked at the bed and back at her. "Some place public. With lots of people."

•

Jesse wasn't sure what was going on. One minute Zach was kissing her like he was going to take her to bed, the next he was dragging her toward the diner. She had to practically jog to keep up with his strides.

"Hey, Zach."

Hearing his name, Zach turned toward the diner parking lot and saw Jimmy.

"Hey man, I was going to come out to the ranch. I needed to talk to you," Jimmy said and looked at Jesse. "Do you have a minute?"

Zach realized he was still holding Jesse's hand. Dropping it, he looked at her. "Go inside and get us a table. I'll be there in a minute."

Still dazed from the kisses, Jesse obeyed and went inside. Looking around she saw an empty booth by the front window and sat down. She could see Zach outside talking to his friend.

*What have I done? I need to tell him the truth even if he is going to kill me.*

"Is this seat taken?"

Jesse looked up to the Bill's smiling blue eyes.

"I talked to Zach. He said you went out to the ranch today," Bill said as he sat down.

"I did," Jesse replied, looking out the window.

"Is he going to be able to help you out?"

Jesse really liked Bill. He was friendly and made her feel like she had known him all her life.

"I'm not sure," she answered, turning to him. "I wasn't exactly honest with him."

"Why's that?"

"Well," Jesse said as she chewed on her lower lip, "when I went to the Triple S, he—" She nodded toward the window. "Was looking at me like I didn't belong here. Like I was a rich city girl who had no idea what a horse even was. I could see in his eyes that he was just being nice to me, I assume, to pacify you." Jesse gave him a half smile. "So when he asked me what I wanted the horses for, I told him I wanted to open a vacation ranch where women could come and mingle with good looking cowboys. I even offered him a job."

When Bill got over the shock of what he'd heard he started laughing. "Hell, I wish I'd been there to see the look on his face."

"It was funny. He just made me so mad the way he was judging me." Jesse's smile faded a little. "But he's going to hate me once he finds out I lied to him, then he'll never help me find the horses I need."

Jesse put her face in her hands and shook her head. Zach Baker did not look like the type of man who would think what she did was funny.

"He'll get over it once he realizes he was wrong to judge you without hearing what you had to say first," Bill said. "Besides, he already knows."

Jesse jerked her head up, "What?"

"He came by the store a little while ago. He said you told him all about your plans. Come to think of it, he was looking at me kind of funny when I told him how great I thought they were."

Jesse slumped in her seat and groaned. "Great."

She'd been here two days and already made an enemy of someone she knew she needed help from.

Maybe there was a slim chance he would accept an apology. The more she knew about him, the easier it would be to get on his good side.

"He was working with two other men, twins. They looked a lot like him. Does he have more children?" Jesse asked playing with the straw in her drink.

"Children? Zach? That would require having a wife. The twins are my great grandsons, Jeremy and Alex. They belong to Zach's brother, Reese." Bill glanced out the window. "Zach came close to marrying once, but it didn't work out. Lisa did a number on his heart, but in the end I think Zach was relieved. They came from different worlds. Broke it off right after Reese's wife left."

Curiosity peaked and Jesse had to ask, "Why'd she leave?" If Reese Baker looked anything like Zach, the woman must have been crazy.

"Wanted to move to the city, couldn't stand being out here where most big cities are over an hour's drive away. She left Reese when the boys were about five."

Jesse looked mortified. How could any mother leave their children no matter how unhappy they were? Jesse thought of Emma and couldn't wait to see her.

"Said she couldn't stand having friends that thought the most exciting event of the year was the rodeo coming to town."

"There's a rodeo?" Jesse asked excitedly.

Bill laughed at her quick change of subject. "Yes. Comes through a few times a year. Should be back in a week or two." Seeing the excitement on her face Bill continued, "We get some big names, too. Bobby Bradley, Hank Jones, Hunter Canyon."

Jesse showed no recognition at any of these names, but her interest didn't diminish. "Do they have bull riding? Broncs? Barrel racing?"

"All that and more."

"I've only seen small rodeos in Connecticut, nothing really exciting. I can't wait to go."

•

When Zach walked into the diner, he immediately saw his grandfather sitting with Jesse frantically waving his arms. Jesse was leaning forward on her elbows and laughing so hard he could see tears in her eyes. Bill was infamous for telling the most outrages stories. Zach only hoped this one was not about him.

"I'll tell you that horse never tried to buck again," he heard his grandfather finish as he walked up.

Laughing, Jesse turned to Zach, her eyes sparkling. The smile she gave him made something inside him say *run*.

"Zach," Bill said, standing, "I was just sharing some old rodeo stories with Jesse. Well, I'll let you two get down to business."

"Good night Bill." Still smiling, Jesse watched Zach slide into the booth across from her. "Your grandfather is a riot."

"I hope the story wasn't too outrageous."

"He had me laughing so hard. Has he really done most of the things he tells people about?" Jessie asked.

Zach smiled and shook his head. "He sure makes you believe he did."

"Why Zach Baker," Sally drawled as she came to the table, "haven't seen you in town for some time."

Jesse noticed Sally's eyes devouring Zach as if he were a piece of chocolate cake.

"Sally," he answered, looking at her.

"What brings you to town?" she said, leaning her hip on the table facing Zach. Sally looked to be about Jesse's age, but her hair was red and it was obvious it was not her natural color.

Zach leaned back in his seat to put distance between them. "Just business."

"Business, huh?" Sally said looking over at Jesse. "Well if you have some time when you're done with your business, you just let me know." Sally gave Jesse a hard look before walking away.

Jesse fiddled with her drink, she could feel Zach staring at her. Not wanting to meet his eyes, she looked around the diner. Luckily, Sally returned with Zach's drink and asked for their order.

"So," he said leaning back and crossing his arms over his chest, "do you want to tell me the real plans for the ranch?"

"I already told you what they were," Jesse said as she sipped her drink.

Zach just glared at her.

The look he was giving her was more than just slightly intimidating. No use pretending since he already knew, she thought.

Jesse sat back and crossed her arms. "Why do I need to tell you? You already know."

"I'd like to hear the truth from you."

"Fine," Jesse huffed. "I plan on building a facility for therapeutic riding. Happy now?"

Zach just raised his eyebrows at her.

"I've researched the area and found there are several barns in the area that host such programs, but most lack the space and horses needed. My facility would put therapeutic riding first, boarders and training second."

"Why therapeutic riding?" he asked.

"Therapeutic riding and hippotherapy are so important to kids with physical and emotional disabilities. Being around the horses allows the kids to be themselves and form a bond with the animals. The horses don't judge them, and love the kids unconditionally. The achievement these kids feel controlling a thousand-pound animal is a great boost to their self esteem."

As Jesse talked about her plans Zach could sense the excitement and passion she felt for the project. He had definitely misjudged her. Her plans were ambitious. A facility the size she was talking about would be a lot of work. He was impressed.

"There are also opportunities to work with soldiers who have been injured."

"Why didn't you tell me all this today?"

She leaned toward him as she spoke. "Because, you expected me to say what I did. Admit it. You think I'm some rich girl from the city, who doesn't know one end of the horse from another." Jesse narrowed her eyes at him and sat back.

Zach had momentarily forgotten he was angry with her. When she leaned toward him, it had given him a wonderful view of her breasts and a glimpse of something lacy.

"You figured my husband had given me a bunch of money to play with so that I would get out of his hair. You thought I would spend a few months here then turn around and leave." Her eyes flashed as she ranted at him.

Jesse gave him her best mean glare. "For your information I don't have, need or want a husband. This ranch will be mine, bought and paid for with my money."

She was right of course, he had thought that. But having heard her real plans and looking at her now he realized he could be in trouble. The kiss that was supposed to have put her in her place did more to him than he wanted to admit. He was actually getting a hard-on while she yelled at him.

Zach grinned to himself, oh the fights they could have and the make-up sex after. A vision of Jesse backed against a wall, legs wrapped around him, ran through his mind.

Jesse looked at him; she couldn't read his face. She wasn't sure what it was about this man. He was intimidating yet she had no fear of him. He seemed to bring out the worst in her.

*Let's not forget how hot he also made you,* she thought.

"What are you smiling at? Why didn't you just tell me you knew I'd lied to you?" she asked.

Zach raised an eyebrow. "Why? You were so enjoying my attempt to get back at you?"

Jesse felt the warmth creep to her face. Not wanting him to know the effect he had on her, she changed the subject.

"Can we just start over?" she asked shyly. "Will you help me find some horses?"

She had gone from angry hellion to needy waif in a matter of seconds. Zach looked at her eyes and felt a pull on his heart he hadn't felt in a long time. She'd caught him off guard today with her vacation ranch remarks. Because she wasn't from here, he'd underestimated her. She'd surprised him and that was rare.

"Yes," he said giving her a soft smile, "I'll help you."

Jesse let her breath out and relaxed.

When Zach smiled his face softened and she noticed small lines around his eyes. She looked at his lips and felt her body heat as she remembered them on hers. She could feel his chest under her hands. Her body was reacting to this man and she couldn't seem to stop it.

This was unfamiliar territory for Jesse. She had never before experienced a physical reaction from just looking at a man. *It's just because he's so good looking,* Jesse thought. *And sexy. And manly. And hot. God, is that steam coming off him?*

Sally brought their food just as Jesse was contemplating crawling over the table and onto Zach's lap.

"So what type of horses do you need exactly?"

"I'll eventually want about ten horses. Breed is not as important as their temperaments. They'll need to be good natured and easy to work around. Not too tall, between fifteen and sixteen hands. I'll need a few ponies also."

*Okay,* Zach thought, *she does know one horse from another.* He told her he might know of a few older horses that needed a good home. Since the ranch had a small barn Jesse could hire someone to help take care of them until the new barn was built.

"Bill said you'd be able to tell me if the contractors I spoke with were reliable."

"Who have you seen so far?"

Jesse gave him the names.

"Don't go with Jones. He'll try to take advantage of you, literally."

Jesse crinkled her nose up. The man had been a bit of a pervert. He kept looking her up and down and licking his lips the whole time he spoke with her. She had already ruled him out, but was glad to hear Zach say it, too.

"Morgan is a good guy. He does good work and hires good people. I've used him for some work at my place."

Jesse already knew this. Mr. Morgan had brought a list of references with him and Zach was on the list.

"That's it so far. I have two more appointments this week," Jesse said.

"Meet with them all," Zach said. "If you end up not liking any of them I'm sure you can find someone in Butte who will come out here for the money it will take for your project."

They ordered coffee and Jesse splurged on apple pie a la mode. Since losing weight, Jesse was more careful not to eat too many sweets. She didn't deny herself, but realized she had previously used food to try and make herself happy.

As she licked the spoon, Jesse wondered if Zach would be interested in helping work off the extra calories from dessert. Mixed in with the impure thoughts of Zach was what Jesse thought was the most brilliant idea.

"Zach, I have an offer for you," Jesse said.

He couldn't help but watch her. Every time she licked the ice cream off the spoon he thought he'd die. Didn't she know how hot that looked? Was it too soon to ask her if she'd like to lick something else?

Zach moved his gaze from her lips to her eyes and hoped it was the same offer he was about to give her.

"Would you be interested in working with me? I'd like to hire you." She paused. "As a consultant."

"Consultant, huh?" Zach said raising an eyebrow.

"Yeah." Jesse went on, "I could really use the help. My knowledge runs more in taking care of horses, not building homes for them. You've already suggested things I hadn't thought of."

*And there are a few things I've thought of that I haven't suggested,* Zach thought.

"I'd pay you of course. And," she said pausing to lick the last bit of ice cream off the spoon, "you said yourself the contractors might try to take advantage of me. If you're working with me they would think twice about doing so."

Zach couldn't resist. Putting his arms on the table he leaned forward. "And how is it you know I won't try and take advantage of you?" he asked, a wicked grin playing on his lips.

Jesse knew what he was doing. She had gotten the best of him today and he had to prove he could play, too. Jesse was more than game. So instead of backing down, Jesse looked into those eyes that made her body weak and imitated him by leaning forward onto the table, bringing her face inches from his.

"I don't," she replied. "But I think I've already proven that I'm equipped to handle one cowboy."

Zach eyes seemed to caress Jesse as he looked from her face to her breast and back up. "Yes, you are equipped."

Jesse couldn't help but think of how much trouble she would be in if he agreed to help her. Something about this man made her feel wicked.

"Besides," Jesse said smiling mischievously, "you taking advantage of me might be very interesting."

If Zach leaned a little farther in, he'd be able to touch his lips to hers. He knew her mouth would taste sweet from eating the pie, but what about the rest of her? He was itching to reach out and run a finger along the top of her breast.

Jesse could feel Zach's breath against her lips. Her heart was beating wildly and her body was responding fully to the man across from her. One word and she would climb across the table onto his lap. *What a way to announce yourself in a new town.*

"Will that be one check or two?"

Zach held Jesse's gaze another second before turning to Sally. "One."

Jesse took a deep breath. She had to control her attraction to Zach or she was going to get herself into a lot trouble.

•

Zach walked her the few blocks back to the hotel.

Stopping, Jesse turned to look up at him. "You never gave me an answer about working with me."

Zach knew it would be a mistake to spend time with her. His attraction when she came out to the ranch, then again tonight, told him she'd be nothing but trouble. But he also knew if he turned her down he'd never hear the end of it from his grandfather. Before he could form the word no, he heard a yes coming out of his mouth.

Jesse almost threw her arms around him, but stopped herself. "Really? Great! I promise to take all your advice seriously, and we can work around your schedule."

Zach had to laugh at her excitement.

"Ah, Zach, one more thing—" She paused with a giant smile still on her face. "Would you be able to teach me to ride?"

"You can't ride and you bought a horse ranch?" Zach asked shaking his head.

Jesse drew her browns together. "Well, of course I can ride, just not western. I grew up riding English style. I can sit in a western saddle. But now that I have all that land, I want to be able to ride on it and be confident. I don't want to worry about not knowing how to control my horse."

"Riding is riding. The styles can't be very different."

"I know that, but I've always ridden in a confined area. I'm a little nervous about riding in the open." She was biting her bottom lip as she waited for his answer.

Zach wasn't sure if she could ride at all. She did look a little nervous and if she got hurt, he'd never forgive himself.

"Sure. I've got some horses you can start on."

Jesse beamed with excitement.

Zach turned to walk back to his truck. Knowing she was watching him, he looked back over his shoulder and smiled at her. When she smiled back, his mind again told him to *run!*

# Chapter Five

*S*he could feel his hands sliding over her skin. She was lying naked on a blanket and the sun was warming her body. Those hands were glorious. Jesse moaned. Rough fingers were circling one nipple, she arched up and felt wetness on the other. She reached up to put her hands in his hair, not allowing him to remove his mouth.

His tongue flicked back and forth making Jesse's breath catch. His mouth was still on her as his hand moved lower. Caressing as it went. He began to rub between her thighs. Running his fingers over her warm spot ever so lightly.

When Jesse lifted her hips, he let his fingers slide in and then slowly out. She couldn't take it. He lifted his head and brought his lips to hers. All the while moving his fingers in and out, torturing her.

Finally he moved his body above hers. She arched up trying to force him into her. She felt the tip of him at her opening and dug her nails into his back in anticipation. When he finally moved into her, she wrapped her legs around his so he couldn't break himself from her. She grabbed at him, helping him move in and out.

He was kissing her neck, her shoulders, all while he moved his hips in a sensual dance. Jesse's breathing quickened. She could feel something so spectacular building in her. She encouraged him to move faster, harder. Finally, her body let go and Jesse screamed, "Zach!"

Jesse woke up breathing very hard. She looked around to

make sure she was still in her hotel room. Alone. She'd had vivid dreams in the past, but this one took the cake.

Jesse could still feel Zach's hands moving over her. His body inside her, the weight of him on her. Jesse frowned. This couldn't be good. Well, maybe. *No, get a grip, Jess. Hey Zach, can you help me learn to ride? Can I start with you?*

•

The phone was ringing. Jesse looked at the clock — 8:45. She grabbed the receiver so whoever was calling would leave her alone. It was the realtor.

"The closing will be Monday at 10:00 AM. They found a local lawyer to handle it so you won't have to go all the way to Butte."

"You've earned every cent of your commission," Jesse said.

"I'll see you Monday unless something comes up and you need me."

Jesse was still sleepy. Every time she closed her eyes last night she had another dream about Zach. She always woke up smiling, but was beginning to worry she was subconsciously obsessed with the man.

The phone rang again, and Jesse pulled the pillow over her head as she grabbed for it. "Hello."

"Jesse?"

Hearing the deep throaty voice she pulled the pillow off her face she shot straight up.

"Hey," he said, "it didn't sound like you for a second."

"People always sound different on the phone." What was she supposed to say? *I had a pillow over my face so I could scream into it every time I had an orgasm while having sex with you in my dreams?*

"What are you doing? Are you busy this afternoon?" Zach asked.

Jesse stretched. "I'm still lying in bed wondering if I feel like getting up."

"Do you have time this afternoon? I have to ride out to check some fences along the property line and thought it would be a good chance for you to ride."

*Hmm, lay in bed all day alone or go riding across the open range with a sexy cowboy. That's a no brainer.*

"Sounds great. What time?"

"Be here around two. We'll be gone a couple hours so don't make any other plans."

"I'll be there," Jesse replied and hung up.

Getting dressed, she wondered lavender or red lingerie. She went with the red. It's not like she thought her dream was going to come true, but it never hurt to be prepared in case her clothes fell off.

Jeans, boots, brown V-neck tee. She wasn't stupid. She saw Zach sneaking glimpses of her breasts last night. It felt good to have someone look at her that way. It made her feel young and alive.

Not knowing how late she would be, she grabbed a sweatshirt on the way out.

As she walked over to the diner, Jesse tried to figure out her attraction to Zach. It was obviously a physical one. Her body immediately responded when she saw him or, thought about him, or like this morning, just heard his voice. His smile made her weak at the knees. Her heart started to pound and the rest of her body just went berserk.

She'd never felt a strong physical attraction like this, had never felt this with her ex-husband. There was no immediate desire when she looked at or thought about Paul, no weak knees—there was nothing.

Jesse had enjoyed flirting with Zach last night, but she didn't come here looking for a relationship, she came here to start a new life. Even if Zach was the most delectable thing she'd ever set her eyes on, she had to stay focused on herself first.

Jen was working so Jesse sat in her section.

"Morning," Jen said as she brought some coffee over. "I guess you decided to look up Zach."

Jesse figured Jen had heard about her dinner with Zach, not

that it was a secret.

"Yeah. We got off to a rough start, but he seems really great. He'll be a big help to me."

"He is great. His nephew Jeremy is my boyfriend."

"One of the twins," Jesse said. "He's very handsome. You must have your hands full keeping the girls away from him," Jesse said, sipping her coffee.

"We've been together since our senior year. I worried at first, but Jeremy gives me no reason to. Let me know if you need anything else."

As Jen walked away, Jesse wondered if she would be so easygoing with a boyfriend who looked like that. *I guess that's what a trusting, open relationship is like.*

# Chapter Six

Zach finished up with the gelding he was working with. It was almost two and Jesse would be here soon. He was having trouble trying to keep her out of his mind. He'd slept poorly last night and woken up several times from dreams of running his hands over her body.

Yes, she was attractive, beautiful even. He liked that she didn't wear a lot of makeup or seem to fuss with her hair. She was a "take me as I am" kind of girl, and he liked that. Nothing fake, no pretenses.

Zach stood in the shower thinking about what to do. He was attracted to Jesse and had agreed to help her. That gave him a reason to spend time with her, like today. He didn't really need to check the fences, but he called and invited her out since she wanted help riding. The fact that he was already coming up with reasons to see her worried him.

He got dressed and walked back toward the barn, thoughts of Jesse following him. He stopped short when he saw her. She was standing in front of his paint gelding, Ty. Her eyes were closed and she was smiling. Ty's nose was against her cheek as he took in her scent. It was one of the most beautiful sights Zach had ever seen. He felt the same tug at his heart that he'd felt last night.

Shaking his head to clear it, he walked toward Jesse. "Right on time."

Jesse turned. She hadn't seen him when she'd first driven up, but she figured he'd eventually show up. She saw the gelding standing there looking at her, and when he whinnied she'd gone over to him. She started out just talking to him, but when he raised his nose to get her scent she almost cried. Bear used to do the same thing. She closed her eyes and for a moment it was as if she'd never given him up.

"Are you okay?" Zach asked. He saw that her checks were wet as if she had been crying.

"Yes, I'm fine. This handsome boy just brought back a special memory for me," Jesse replied, patting Ty one more time.

"Would you like to ride him?"

With a worried look Jesse asked, "Do you think I could handle him?" He wasn't a big horse and had a kind face, but Jesse was wary of any horse she didn't know.

"Ty's pretty easygoing. He'll take care of you," Zach said, grabbing the halter.

After putting him on the cross ties, he showed Jesse where the brushes were so she could start cleaning him up while he got Star.

Zach watched as Jesse brushed Ty and picked out his hooves, the whole time talking to him. She seemed to know what she was doing, so he knew she wasn't lying about having been around horses. He had to smile at the way she was trying to convince Ty she was a beginner and he should go easy on her.

Zach brought the saddles out and showed Jesse how to fit the saddle to the horse and girth it up. They lead the horses out of the barn and Zach made sure Jesse was able to get on Ty before he mounted Star. Although a little awkward, Jesse pulled herself into the saddle and smiled proudly.

They started off at a walk going east. Zach wanted to show Jesse where their property met. It was one of the prettiest places in this area.

"Let me know if you get tired. Once you ask Ty to go forward, try to keep your leg off him or he'll think you want him to go faster," Zach said. Jesse nodded. She was used to keeping her leg pressed against the horse for both his support and hers, not keeping them relaxed.

Zach picked up the trot and Jesse felt as if she was just pounding on poor Ty's back.

"Just relax. Let your hips move with him."

Jesse tried. She relaxed her hips and back, and tried to move with Ty instead of sitting so rigid. She hated that she had to hold onto the saddle horn for support. When Zach picked up a slow canter, Jesse was relieved. This motion she had down. Jesse smiled at Zach. This was a wonderful feeling. Nothing but open space ahead and behind. She would never want to ride in an enclosed ring again.

•

They had been riding for about an hour when Zach stopped at the top of a hill. Jesse looked to the valley below and could hear the river. It went on for miles until it twisted out of sight behind the mountains beyond.

Dismounting, Jesse just stood in awe of the sight.

"That's your ranch," Zach said smiling.

"You're kidding, right?" Jesse could not believe she owned such a beautiful thing. She sat down and just stared.

"If you keep going east, you'll eventually come to the house and barn. This is the back side of the land," he said, sitting down beside her.

Jesse turned to him, a wide smile on her face. "It's more beautiful than I could ever have imagined. It's inspiring,"

Zach smiled. The look on Jesse's face was definitely worth the ride out here.

Totally at ease with Zach, Jesse leaned back on her arms and closed her eyes. She was happy. They both seemed to have put yesterday behind them. Zach had been nothing but pleasant and friendly today.

*I could get used to spending time with him*, Jesse thought. Her physical attraction to him was one thing, but there was something else about him she couldn't put her finger on.

Zach watched as Jesse looked out in appreciation of the

land. She seemed to truly love being here, just like he did. He let his eyes roam over her.

Her hair was loose and the light wind was blowing it back from her face. Zach's eyes moved down. He couldn't help but stare at the way her neck was exposed. Her skin looked silky soft. He could see a piece of red lace peaking out of her shirt. The urge to touch her, to run kisses down her neck to the top of her breast, was strong.

"You know Zach," she said, sitting up and turning to him. "I was thinking."

*So was I*, he thought as he watched her mouth.

"I think I should come and do some work on your ranch."

Zach brought his eyes to hers. "You want to work on the ranch?"

"Yeah. It would be a great way for me to learn about ranching." Jesse smiled like this was the best idea in the world. "You wouldn't have to pay me. I'd do it for the experience."

Zach looked at her like she was nuts. Having Jesse work at the ranch would be a very bad idea. He'd never get anything done. Besides having thoughts all day about what type of experience he'd like to give her, he would worry about her getting hurt.

"I don't know if that's such a good idea," he said, running his hands through his hair.

"Why not?"

She just didn't seem to get it. At this moment he was thinking about lying her on the ground and welcoming her to the neighborhood.

"Jesse, ranch work is hard. You get up early, the days are long—"

"But it would be a great way for me to learn. I don't need to spend all day, everyday here." She was looking at him with pleading eyes. "Just if there was something going on that might be a benefit to me to learn."

Zach was still not sure this would be a great idea, but heard himself saying yes once again.

Jesse screamed and threw her arms around his neck. "You won't regret it, I promise." Her smile was so big Zach couldn't help but smile back and hope she was right.

Her face was just inches from his. Jesse's breath caught as his eyes met hers. Her arms were around his neck, his around her waist. He wanted to kiss her. She could see it in his eyes that he was looking for the okay.

Jesse brought her face closer to his so that their lips were barely touching. She hoped that was enough.

It was.

His lips meet hers in a soft, sensual kiss. Jesse's heartbeat went from zero to a hundred. She had never been kissed in such a way. It was slow and deliberate and very arousing.

Zach was quickly getting accustomed to kissing Jesse. She had sighed into his mouth as if this was the best kiss she'd ever had. He was enjoying himself immensely.

He felt like a teenager who was with a girl for the first time. Although he wanted to explore her body, he was perfectly content just kissing her.

Separating their lips, Zach rested his forehead against hers as he got his emotions under control. He was used to casual relationships, and this would be no different. So why was it he wished he could stay out here forever?

"Look," he said, pointing to the right of where they sat. Jesse gasped. An eagle had landed on a large boulder not more than a few hundred feet from them.

The eagle proudly held its head high as it looked around. It was magnificent. Letting out a loud screech, it spread its wings and flew away.

Jesse was sure she was going to die of excitement.

"Did you see him? He was gorgeous. Do they come here a lot? I have to come back and take pictures." She had gotten up and was peering over the cliff where the eagle had flown.

"Don't lean over too far," Zach said, grabbing her arm.

When she turned to him, Zach could see the pure joy on her face. All from seeing an eagle. Zach shook his head. Her excitement over these simple things would be his downfall. He was in trouble and was about to get in deeper.

"Why don't you stay for dinner?" he asked as he and Jesse walked with him back to the horses. "I usually get some deer and on occasion a bear roaming around."

"Really?" Jesse said excitedly.

Normal women ran from the thought of deer and bear roaming around their homes.

Zach smiled. "Really."

# Chapter Seven

*T*aking a drink from his beer, Zach watched as Jesse threw the ball for his dog Luke.

"He'll make you keep going all night if you let him."

Jesse smiled. She had dirty paw prints all over her but didn't seem to care, and the ball had to be covered with dog slobber by now.

"Come on, dinner's about ready. And you're not allowed at the table with dog spit all over you."

Jesse came up the stairs and into the house. Luke following behind her. "Bathroom is down the hall to the left," he said, placing plates on the table.

Jesse walked down the hall looking in the other rooms as she went. There was an office to the left and just past it another room that held some exercise equipment. Past that was a guest bedroom across from the bathroom. Beyond that at the end the house was the master bedroom. Jesse went into the bathroom and washed up.

When she came out her curiosity got the best of her. She was dying to know what Zach's bedroom looked like. *Face it,* she told herself, *you want to see where he sleeps.*

So instead of turning right and going back to the kitchen, she turned left, looking over her shoulder like a bandit.

The room was beautiful. There was a king-size bed to the left. The headboard was made from what looked to be carved tree logs, and had a turquoise and tan colored blanket on it. There was a door to the left of the bed that looked like it led to a bathroom. Peeking in, Jesse noticed the colors in the bathroom were similar to the blanket. The tile was a tan, but there were turquoise ones scattered on the floor and shower. But the most magnificent thing about the bedroom had to be the view.

The bed faced a wall of windows that looked out to the mountains beyond. The house must be raised in the back because Jesse noticed a deck. How wonderful would it be to wake up to that view every day? Jesse wondered.

"Beautiful, isn't it?"

Jesse jumped at the sound of his voice, her face reddening a little. She was so taken by the view, she hadn't heard Zach come down the hall.

"I'm sorry. I didn't mean to snoop. But I saw the windows and couldn't help looking."

Zach smiled because he understood. He had the windows installed after he bought the ranch. The view was too spectacular not to be able to see it from inside the house.

Jesse looked out the windows again. "I'd love to do something like this at my ranch. I want to be able to see the mountains from everywhere in the house."

Zach watched Jesse look out at the mountains. When he first realized where she was, he'd gotten a little annoyed. But his annoyance left quickly when he saw her standing in front of the windows, the light from the sunset on her, a small smile on her face. Her smile, he realized, said a lot about her. When she smiled softly, just a small smile, it said how much she truly liked something.

She looked at him and when her eyes met his, they told him she appreciated the view as much as he did.

Jesse looked at Zach and realized it was getting a little hot in the room. He was standing with his arms crossed, leaning on the door frame. His shirt was pulled across his chest and his jeans seemed to be riding a little lower on his hips than usual. He was gorgeous, there was no denying it.

"The best part of the day is waking up and just lying in bed looking out the windows," he said with his eyes still on her.

"I bet it is."

She couldn't stop looking at him. For an instant she pictured him walking toward her, taking her face in his hands and kissing her as he did today. Jesse's knees felt weak from the thought.

And although she tried not to, Jesse glanced to the bed then back at Zach. She could feel herself willing Zach to walk to her.

The way she was looking at him told Zach he could have her right now without protest. His body was responding just to the thought. Working with her was not going to be easy.

"Guess we should eat before Luke jumps on the table and makes off with our dinner," he said, breaking the silence.

Jesse took a breath. "Yeah, I'm starving," she said as she moved toward him. Because he didn't move, Jesse brushed against him. Pausing for a moment, she closed her eyes to the rush of heat she felt when their skin touched. Letting out a breath, she continued down the hall.

•

Dinner was fantastic. Jesse never had a man cook for her before. The steak was perfect and she even had some wine. She wasn't much of a drinker, but she figured one glass would be okay. And after what she felt in the bedroom, she needed something to help steady herself.

"Did you grown up in Montana?" Jesse asked.

"Yes, couple of towns from here. My mother still lives there. My father passed away a few years ago."

They were still sitting at the table, plates uncleared. Zach leaned back in his chair, stretched his legs out, and crossed them at the ankles. *Dessert anyone?* she thought.

"I'm sorry to hear that." Both of Jesse's parents were still alive and she dreaded the thought of losing either of them.

"It was hard for my mom. They had been together since high school. He was the only life she knew." Jesse could see that Zach still hurt from losing his father.

"Were you close to him?"

"Yes. He was a hard man sometimes. My brother and I drove him crazy." Zach smiled as he thought about his dad. "He taught Reese and me how to ride, rope, fish, just about everything. I was glad I was able to buy this ranch before he passed. I wanted him to know I was here because of everything he taught me."

"Is it just you and your brother?" Jesse asked, sipping at her wine.

"No, we have a younger sister. I'm in the middle. Kelly is married and lives near my mother, which works out well since she has young kids, and that helps keep my mom busy."

Jesse sat back and listened to Zach talk about his family. By the tone of his voice they seemed to be close. She could hear the love in his words when he spoke about them.

"How about you?" he asked. "Where's your family?"

"I'm the youngest of three kids. I have a brother and sister who still live in Connecticut near my mom and dad."

"What brought you out to Montana?" Zach asked. Montana was a long way from the east coast. If she had lived in the city, what had made her move to a ranch in the middle of nowhere?

Jesse looked at her wine and swirled it in the glass. She had nothing to hide, but wasn't sure how much she wanted to talk about her past. She was hurt and embarrassed by her failed marriage and wanted to put it behind her.

"I needed an adventure, someplace new. I knew I didn't belong in Connecticut. I felt—" Jesse paused. How could she explain that she felt she was not living her destiny, that she knew her life was meant to be more than what it was? "I felt like something was missing. I would look around and feel like I was in the wrong place. That I wasn't home."

Jesse looked out the windows at the mountains. "I felt like my life had been a bunch of wrong turns. That I never really followed my heart, but tried to be something I wasn't instead. I went through my days always thinking there had to be something more."

Looking at Zach, Jesse realized how comfortable she was with him. She felt like she could tell him anything and he would understand.

"I can understand how you feel," he said. "After high school, I went to college. I worked in the city for awhile." Taking a drink of his beer he went on. "Working in an office just wasn't for me. I felt I was in the wrong place, that I wasn't home."
His time in the city was something he had put behind him. What he had felt for Lisa had made him move there.

Jesse giggled behind her wine.

"What?" he asked. He was getting a little buzzed and Jesse was looking even better in the moonlight than she did in the sun.

"I was just picturing you in a suit, behind a desk and wondering if you'd still look as hot as you do in your jeans." Jesse's clamped her mouth shut. She could *not* believe she'd just said that out loud.

"Hot, huh?" Zach grinned like a Cheshire cat.

It was a smoldering grin that told Jesse she was in trouble. Her one glass of wine had turned into two. If she wasn't careful she'd wake up looking at that view of the mountains from his bed.

"I should help you clean up," Jesse said, standing so quickly she bumped the table.

Zach watched her walk to the sink. He finished his beer and stood up to follow her. Standing behind her, he reached around to place the dishes in the sink. His body was barely touching hers, but the heat he felt made it feel like they were pressed together.

Jesse froze. She could feel Zach up against her—all she had to do was lean back. If she turned he would have her pinned against the counter. Even though they were alone and miles from town she was not afraid of him, at least not in the sense she thought he would hurt her.

When she felt him push her hair aside, and his lips touched her neck, she had to lean into the counter. Her body again tingled from head to toe.

As Zach trailed kisses up her neck to her ear, she closed her eyes to the feeling. She felt herself being turned to face him and could do nothing to stop him even if she wanted to. As she turned, his lips never left her skin until they found her lips. When his tongue slid into her mouth, her arms slid around his neck. Her body took over, her mind no longer in control.

The kiss was like the one on the mountain. Soft and exploring, like he was trying to taste her, get the feel of her. When he leaned into her, she could feel his hardness through his jeans. God she wanted him, but this wasn't right. If she slept with him, she could ruin the new life she was trying to make. Her body was screaming at her mind to shut up, but in the end her mind won out.

Jesse pulled away and walked over to the table. She had to put distance between her and Zach. "I need to go."

She could see the passion in his eyes, the heat in his look, and knew this would have been an incredible night.

"I'm sorry, it's just—"

Zach raked his hand through his hair. "No, it's okay. I'll walk you out." Zach started to move away from the counter.

"No," Jesse screamed. If he came anywhere near her she'd rip his clothes off.

Zach stopped. "Are you okay to drive?" he asked.

Jesse nodded yes.

"Call me when you get back to the hotel."

"Okay, I will." She turned and almost tripped trying to get out so fast.

Zach watched her leave. "Luke old boy, I think I need a cold shower."

•

Jesse didn't want to call him when she reached the hotel, but she knew he'd worry if she didn't. *He must think I am a complete loser.* She knew that sleeping with him would not have been the right thing to do, but she couldn't deny her body came alive whenever he touched her.

Her sex life in the past had been horrible. She had only a few partners before her husband, but with all of them, including her husband, sex was something she dreaded.

She had always thought there was something wrong with her. She couldn't understand why she was so turned off by the mere thought of sex. Eventually she realized it wasn't sex itself, it was who she was having sex with. Although Paul was good looking and fit, she just wasn't attracted to him. Looks, she realized, were only part of the attraction when you felt something for someone.

Jesse believed she would someday find someone who would ignite a passion in her like she'd never known.

Zach made her body feel alive. She wanted to feel his hand on her, wanted him to touch her. Why was he so different? He was good looking, had a great body, fantastic smile, but she'd seen all that before and never reacted the way she had tonight.

She picked up the phone and dialed.

"I made it."

"You could have stayed. The view out the bedroom window is really something to wake up to."

His voice was low and husky.

"Maybe next time, cowboy."

Jesse sighed as she hung up the phone. She looked at her empty bed, then pictured Zach on his bed with jeans on, no shirt, and the moonlight coming through the windows. She couldn't believe she'd left.

# Chapter Eight

*J*esse didn't hear from Zach the next day. She had appointments with the remaining contractors on her list so she was occupied for most of the day. But she started to worry just a little when she didn't hear from him the following day either.

Thoughts started running through Jesse's head. Maybe he wasn't attracted to her. No, that couldn't be. *A man doesn't kiss someone like that if there is no attraction, do they?* Jesse wasn't sure. Had he been using her? Thinking she was easy because she was new in town? *I should never have kissed him. I don't even know him.* She would just have to keep control of herself when she was around him.

Maybe later she could try and pursue something with him, but for now she had to concentrate on getting settled. *Yeah right.* Jesse knew that the next time she saw Zach it was going to be hard to keep her hands off him.

*What to do*, Jesse thought. Picking up the phone, she dialed. *I need a little help with this.* She listened to the phone ring.

"Hello."

Jesse smiled as she heard her friend's voice. She and Sharon had been friends for more than twenty years. They had met during their much younger days when they both were in love with musicians from a local band.

Sharon was someone Jesse had laughed and cried with, shared all her secrets with. She was the only one who had known that Jesse had wanted to leave Paul, and was always there to listen.

"Hey, it's me."

"Jesse," Sharon said. "Please tell me you're on your way home."

Jesse laughed. "No, but I'll buy you a ticket to come here."

"You'd have to have something pretty spectacular there to get me to come all the way across the country. How's the new town?"

Jesse could hear kids screaming in the background and smiled. "The new town is perfect. It's exactly what I was looking for. The ranch I found is perfect, too."

"What about the people?"

"They seem pretty friendly so far. Some a little more friendly than others," Jesse said, hoping her friend would get the hint.

"How friendly are we talking?"

"Well," Jesse paused, twisting the phone cord around her finger.

"Spill it, Jesse," Sharon said.

"Okay fine. There's this one guy; he's my neighbor."

"And?" Sharon waited.

"He's so unbelievably hot," Jesse gushed, sounding like a teenager.

"So you called me to tell me about your hot neighbor?" Sharon laughed. "Okay, how hot is unbelievably hot?"

"Hot enough to make me feel things I never felt." Jesse paused.

"Really? Do tell."

Jesse could hear the smile in Sharon's voice.

"You know I had no intention of ever going near a man again."

"Yeah."

"But Zach, that's his name, well there's something about him. Sharon, I can't explain how I feel when I'm around him. Just thinking about him makes my body goes wild. When I shook the guy's hand, my panties got wet. And when I kissed him the first time—"

"Wait, the first time. How many times have you kissed

him?"

"Um." Jesse hesitated. "Three or so times." Jesse could feel her body getting warm just talking about Zach. "Sharon, it was amazing. It was like my body was on fire and I was feeling for the first time."

Jesse could hear her friend laughing on the other end of the line.

"Hey. I'm trying to explain my problem to you and you're laughing?" But she was laughing, too.

"I'm sorry," Sharon said, still chuckling. "It's just not like you to describe a non-repulsive attraction to a man. Sounds to me like you're hot for this guy."

"Ya think?" Jesse sighed.

"You should be happy. It sounds as if you finally found someone who will probably make you scream like—"

"Sharon!"

"What? Jesse, seriously, I'm still not sure what your problem is. For years you wished you could find someone who made you feel exactly what you're feeling now."

"I know, but—"

"But what. You don't have to make a lifelong commitment to the guy. You're forty and single. Enjoy yourself. Let him enjoy you."

"You really think so?" Jesse asked sitting on the bed.

"Yes. As long as the guy is not a wacko, I say go for it. What do you have to lose, except your voice from all the screaming you'll be doing."

Sharon said exactly what Jesse had been thinking. She just needed to hear it from someone else so she would feel better.

"You're the best, you know," Jesse said, a little sadness in her voice. "Promise you'll come visit soon?"

"Only if your cowboy has a friend."

•

Still a little concerned that Zach hadn't called, Jesse decided to go by the feed store and see Bill. She wasn't about to tell him about the kisses she and Zach had shared, but she might be able to get some information out of him.

Jesse walked into the store and, not seeing Bill, headed for the clothing section. She loved wearing her comfortable T-shirts, but wanted to pick up a few western-style blouses. She browsed through the racks and held different shirts against herself in the mirror.

"The red one suits you," she heard from behind her. Turning, Jesse found herself looking into a pair of green eyes surrounded by long black lashes.

She had definitely picked the right town to move to. Even if she wasn't looking for a man, it was always nice to know there were several very hot ones around.

A black Stetson sat on top of black hair that just touched the tops of his shoulders. His skin was the color of caramel. He was about the same height as Zach, with a slightly slimmer build, but Jesse could tell that build was all muscle.

He wore what seemed to be the normal cowboy wear of jeans and boots, but he also wore what Jesse recognized as a rodeo belt buckle. She wasn't familiar with what each buckle stood for, but she knew that if you had one you were usually pretty good.

Giving her the most fantastic smile, he held out his hand, "Hunter Canyon."

"Jesse," she replied taking his hand.

As good looking as he was, Jesse noticed that shaking his hand did not have the same effect as Zach's did.

"So, the red huh?" Jesse asked holding it up again.

The shirt in question was actually white, but had a pattern of red flowers on it. It was the one she had been leaning toward.

"What about this one?" Jesse said holding up a blue one and facing him.

"That one would work, too."

Jesse decided she'd take both of them. "Would you mind if I asked for your opinion on one more thing?"

"Certainly," Hunter responded.

Jesse got the impression Hunter was very comfortable with

himself and women. She knew his type—he walked a little too confidently and his smile was a little too inviting.

Jesse walked toward the hat section. Zach had given her a hat the day they rode, but she wanted one of her own. Bill came up to them as they reached the hats.

"Jesse, I thought I saw you come in," Bill said. He looked over at Hunter. "How's the circuit treating you?"

Hunter grinned. "Treating me just fine."

"Hunter is one of the top bull riders in the country," Bill explained. "Got several championships."

"That so," Jesse said, sounding impressed. As she studied the different hats, Bill watched as Hunter studied her. "The brown one I think. What do you think, Bill?"

"Perfect. No one will ever know you haven't lived here all your life," Bill said

"Liar," Jesse said laughing.

"Well, I'll leave you to finish looking around," Bill said. "Hunter, see you in a few weeks."

"Bill," Hunter replied, tipping his hat.

"Are you in town for long?" Jesse asked as she looked through the other racks of clothes. If he was a bull rider he probably spent most of his time traveling.

"For just a few days. Then I'll be back for the rodeo in two weeks," Hunter said as his gaze traveled over her.

Jesse couldn't wait. "How far is the rodeo from here?"

Ending his appraisal, he looked to her face when she turned toward him. "About an hour away, just outside Butte. Are you going?"

"I'd like to," Jesse said.

"Well, make sure you look for me. I'll give you a behind-the-scenes tour."

"Really? That would be great."

Hunter gave her another fantastic smile and tipped his hat before he walked away. Watching him, Jesse wondered what they fed their boys here.

Still wanting to ask Bill about Zach she made her way to the counter.

"Find what you wanted?" Bill asked.

"For now. Bill," she started, not sure what exactly to say, "I haven't heard from Zach and I wanted to talk to him about the other contractors I spoke with. I'd like to make a decision so we can start working on the plans."

"He went out of town, should be back tonight. Had to haul a horse over to Poison. Anything I can help you with?"

"No. I mean not that I don't want your help. It's just, Zach already knows all the plans, and—"

"No need to explain. I understand," Bill said. Jesse blushed. She was sure Bill somehow knew about the other night.

"Thanks, Bill." Taking her purchases she waved as she headed for the door.

Jesse left the feed store feeling much better. So Zach wasn't trying to avoid her, he was just out of town, but he still could have called.

Picking up dinner on the way back to the hotel, Jesse got out her cell phone and dialed. Hearing Zach's voice at the other end got her heart beating. Trying to sound calm and relaxed, she left her message.

"Hey Zach, it's Jesse. Could you give me a call tomorrow? I was hoping we could meet if you have time."

Hanging up, Jesse took a breath. Why was she feeling so nervous? She wasn't chasing this guy. Sure she wanted him to like her, but they were just going to work together some.

She was an adult and she should be able to control these teenage feelings. *Yeah right.*

# Chapter Nine

*J*esse walked into the diner Saturday morning feeling refreshed. She had slept well and had a full day planned. She decided that she would drive over to Butte to find some furniture. She also needed some kitchen and bathroom items since her own things wouldn't arrive until the end of next week.

Seeing Jen, Jesse made her way over to the counter.

"This is Jeremy," Jen said proudly. Jesse hadn't gotten a good look at the Baker twins that day at Zach's ranch, but she got one now. He had the same hair and eye color as Zach, and Jesse knew from seeing him shirtless, the same great body. His smile was warm and friendly, and showed his love for Jen when he looked at her.

Jesse liked him immediately.

"Pleasure to finally meet you," Jeremy said. "Jen's told me a lot about your plans for the ranch."

"Well then, you know I'll need some help. Zach tells me you and your brother sometimes hire out as ranch hands."

"We do. Just let Jen know and she'll put you in touch."

"I will. It was nice meeting you."

As Jesse made her way to her regular booth she said hello to some of the regulars she'd met. When she turned away from saying good morning, she realized there was already someone sitting in her booth.

Her heart stopped when Zach smiled at her. *It's a sin how gorgeous he is.* Just seeing him brought back the heat she'd felt the other night. *Get a grip Jess, walk over there.*

"You're in my booth," she said, placing her hands on her hips.

Zach's eyes twinkled. "I was here first."

*Those eyes*, Jesse thought, *I could stare at them all day.*

"This guy giving you trouble Jesse? I'll take him outside if you want," Jake, one of the regulars, asked.

"I think I can handle this one."

"Alright, but I'll be keeping a close eye on you," he said to Zach.

Jesse laughed and sat down.

•

Having to trailer the colt over to Poison had helped give Zach some time to think. He was really attracted to Jesse, but what man wasn't attracted to a nice looking woman? When he had dinner with her the first night he realized she was more than just looks. She had a plan for her ranch and a lot of ambition.

*I like my life the way it is*, he thought. *I liked the peace and quiet of the ranch. I like doing what I want, when I want. I also like Jesse.*

When he heard her message he was more than excited that she had called, and tempted to call her back despite what time it was.

When she came into the diner, he was able to watch her since she didn't know he was there. It was obvious that the people liked her and she was making friends. How could you not like her? She had a great attitude, always gave a quick smile.

Zach looked at her as she ordered and felt a pang of jealousy as he thought of her with Hunter.

His grandfather had told him about them meeting in his store. "Hunter seemed quite taken with Jesse. But then you know how he is; he's taken with most women."

Yes, Zach knew how Hunter was with women. They'd trip over themselves trying to get his attention, always had, then he'd pick one or two out to follow him around. He didn't think Jesse would be interested in a guy like Hunter, but Zach wasn't sure.

"I got your message and thought I'd see if I could catch you here. What are your plans for today?"

"I thought I'd drive up to Butte. I need to start looking for some furniture," Jesse said. "I close on the house Monday and want to be able to stay there. So it's either look for furniture or buy a sleeping bag and sleep on the floor."

"Want some company?" he asked. "There are a few places I use for supplies. I could show you around."

•

Jesse debated. She really did need to find some furniture, and Zach would be a huge distraction. *But distractions can be good …*

"I'll make a deal with you," she said, "come with me to pick out some furniture and we can stop at the supply stores, too. If you give me opinions I think are good, I'll buy you lunch."

Zach had some things to do out at the ranch, but nothing that couldn't wait until later. "Sure. I can't let you decorate that house in a city retro style."

"City retro," Jesse said with an appalled look on her face. "No way. I want it to be rustic and homey. Picture this—a soft leather couch and chair, light wooden coffee table, big screen TV in the corner, and a fur rug so when I want to lay naked in front of the fire I have something soft to lay on."

Zach choked on his coffee.

Jesse grinned. She'd gotten exactly the response she wanted.

•

Zach pulled into the parking lot of the furniture store Jen had recommended to Jesse. They scanned the aisles finding a couch and chair Jesse liked. When the saleswoman approached, she went directly to Zach and ignored Jesse. Jesse couldn't blame her; she would have done the same.

While Zach showed the saleswoman the furniture Jesse was interested in and inquired about delivery, she wandered into the bedroom section. When Jesse turned to see if Zach was following, she saw him staring down at a fur rug on the floor.

He looked up at her with raised eyebrows. Jesse met his gaze.

Jesse bounced up and down on different mattresses, trying to determine which one would be most comfortable.

"Zach," she called, still bouncing, "come and lay on this one and tell me what you think."

Zach groaned.

"You're sure you want me to lie down?" he asked. She noticed his eyes had changed to the grey-blue they'd been the other night when they had kissed.

Jesse wasn't going to let him know he was getting to her. "Sure, why not?" she asked innocently. She scooted over. With the sides of their bodies touching, they laid there looking up at the ceiling.

"Feels fine to me," he said.

"Well, I had to be sure since beds aren't just for sleeping."

He turned his face toward her. "That so."

Jesse turned her head to face him, her eyes looking into his, her heart racing. Then, taking her friend's advice, she sat up and threw her leg over Zach, straddling him.

"There are other things that require the bed to be comfortable and sturdy."

His lips twitched. "Really?"

Jesse's experience in seduction was limited, but she was going to give it her all.

"Yes, some people like to watch TV in bed," she said, placing her hands beside his head and lowering her face close to his. "I personally enjoy reading in bed."

"Reading, huh?"

Blue eyes met brown.

There was a noise in the distance as Zach moved his lips toward hers. Someone was talking to them. Couldn't they see he was busy?

Jesse pulled her lips away just as Zach's touched hers, to see the saleswoman standing there.

"Um, I'll take this one," she said, climbing off Zach.

The saleswoman just walked away. Jesse turned to smile at

him, then walked off to pay.

On the way back to Dillon they stopped at the stores Zach had mentioned. As they walked around, he pointed out items he thought she might find useful once her barn was built.

He introduced her to the store owners and she explained her plans and items she was interested in.

Zach watched Jesse interact with the owners and was impressed with the questions she asked about some of the products. He also noticed how the store owners looked at Jesse. She was friendly and beautiful and Zach was sure they saw her as free game. Although he shouldn't care, he did. He felt a possessiveness toward Jesse that, oddly, he wasn't entirely uncomfortable with.

When they stopped for lunch, Zach asked about her daughter. Jesse missed Emma, but she wanted to have everything in place before she came out.

"I'll go and get her in a month or so. I want everything in place before she gets her so I can spend time with her exploring and getting used to living someplace new."

"How old is she?"

"She just turned seven a few months ago. She's not very happy about coming here. She didn't want to leave her friends and doesn't understand why her father isn't coming."

She remembered how upset Emma had gotten when she found out they were selling their house and moving. She wouldn't come out of her room for two days. Jesse finally decided to send her to her grandparents for a visit while she came and looked for houses.

"She'll settle in and make new friends. Kids are tough. Before long she won't even be thinking about Connecticut."

"I know." Jesse paused. "The divorce, the move—it's a lot for her. I just want her to be happy."

"She'll be fine, you'll see."

Jesse smiled and wondered how Emma was going to react to their new neighbor. Because he was helping her, Zach would be spending a good bit of time over at the ranch. She hoped

Emma didn't think Jesse was trying to replace her dad.

# Chapter Ten

*J*esse sat on the deck outside her new home. The closing had gone smoothly. The funds had been transferred and the lawyers were happy.

Afterward, Jesse had driven to Butte and loaded up on items she needed for the next few days before finally heading to her house. The furniture was delivered that afternoon and she set about putting her things away. With almost everything done, she made some dinner and came out to the deck.

She was really proud of herself. She'd done what she said she was going to do. Her life was on the path she thought it should be on and she was finally happy. She was finally living the life she was meant to live.

With the riding school she'd be helping people as well as be around the horses she loved. She was making friends and so far loved the town.

Jesse was still sitting out on the deck an hour later when Zach came walking around the house. He'd knocked but didn't get an answer, so walked around back to find her.

Since she had no outdoor furniture, Jesse was sitting on the stairs. When she saw him, she looked up and smiled.

"All settled in?" he asked.

"Yes. It was a busy day, but worth it."

Zach held up a bottle of wine. "To welcome you to the neighborhood."

It had been a long day and wine sounded just like the thing to help her unwind. She got up and went inside to get some glasses.

"I hope these will do," she said, lifting up some mugs. "I'm not prepared for entertaining."

"They'll work fine," he said, pulling a bottle opener from his pocket.

"You think of everything," Jesse said, nudging him with her shoulder. "Now I know who to come to if I need a cup of sugar."

Zach looked around at the furniture. When he looked past the couch to the fireplace his eyes settled on the fur rug in front of it. Jesse looked in the same direction.

"What? It matches the couch," she said, laughing. Jesse grabbed her mug and went back outside.

Sitting, Zach saw two gray fur balls come running out of the house. At first he thought they were rats, but they jumped into Jesse's lap and he saw they were kittens.

Scooping them up, Jesse held them to her face and smiled. "My first rescuees. These are Romeo and Juliet."

She'd passed the local animal shelter on her way back from town and couldn't resist stopping. There were so many animals. Dogs and cats, young and old. Jesse didn't want to get any dogs until hers arrived and were settled in. But she couldn't resist the kittens. One meow from them and she was gone.

Jesse pet the kittens and looked Zach over. She wasn't sure what to make of him. Guys this nice only existed in the movies. But here he was with her—intelligent, caring, thoughtful and sexy as hell. She sensed he had a stubborn streak, but without the arrogance. It had been a long time since anyone cared about her thoughts and ideas. He made her feel like she could do anything just by listening to her.

"You look lost," Zach said.

"Hm. I was just thinking about the past week and how my life has changed in such a short time. I really feel like moving here was the right thing to do."

"You had doubts?" Zach asked.

"Wouldn't you?" Jesse replied. "When I finally realized my life wasn't what I wanted it to be, moving across the country wasn't the first thought that entered my mind."

The wine was kicking in and since her family thought she was crazy, she wanted someone to understand why she was here.

"My marriage was not what a marriage should be, or at least how I wanted it to be. I shouldn't have gotten married, not to Paul anyway. I could tell he wasn't what I wanted in a husband before we got married, but I'd been with him so long it just seemed like the thing to do. He wasn't abusive or an alcoholic, so I could've done worse. But he wasn't supportive—very self-centered and he wasn't a good partner."

Jesse took a sip of her wine and realized Zach had been more supportive of her in one week than Paul had been in all the years they were together.

"After Emma was born, I thought he would be better," she went on. "I'd hoped he'd help around the house, with the baby, that sort of thing. But he didn't. He'd get mad because I was always tired, not realizing I did more than just go to work and come home. I had a baby to take care of, a house and bills to manage, and try to be a wife, too. He liked to go out—I was over that. I enjoyed staying home. He would tell me I needed to get out more, but when I finally did, he was mad because I wasn't home."

Zach just sat and listened.

"I started to ride again. Made friends at the barn. Went to horse shows. It's what I enjoyed doing. He was glad I found something I liked, but as I spent more time with the horses, he didn't like it so much anymore. Then I bought Bear."

"Bear?"

Jesse looked down at the kittens now asleep in her lap.

"A friend approached me about buying a horse and retraining him. I said yes. I thought it would be a way to help me pay off some of the debt that was holding me back."

Jesse smiled at the memory. "Bear turned out to be a lot

of fun. He had the greatest personality ever. He was lazy sometimes, but would step up if you asked him, and he never got angry. He became a fantastic horse and I fell in love with him." Jesse closed her eyes and could see the horse clearly in her mind.

"That's who Ty reminded you of that day you came to ride?" Zach asked.

"Yes. He belonged to me, and me to him. I tried to figure out ways to keep him, but I couldn't afford to." Jesse looked at him, her eyes moist. "Never in my life had I felt like I'd let anyone down like I felt I'd let him down." Jesse felt her heart breaking all over again. "He depended on me, loved me, no questions asked. He listened to me when I needed someone to listen. His eyes, those big brown trusting eyes." Jesse looked down, her shoulders shaking slightly.

"My ex owned a classic Mustang. He had bought it the year after Emma was born. Said he had always wanted one to restore; it would make him so happy to own it. I don't know how many times I looked at that car and thought if we sold it, I could keep my horse. But the thought never entered his mind. It was a status symbol to him. He would never give up something of his for someone else." Jesse closed her eyes and shook her head. "God I hated that car."

Jesse looked toward the barn and went on. "I used to think material things would make me happy. A nice car, a big house, but I had those things and I was miserable. I was in debt because of it and stuck in my marriage because of the debt. And because of it all, I had to give up the thing I truly loved. The day Bear sold, my heart broke."

Jesse wiped her cheek where tears had slipped down.

"Now's probably not the best time to tell you that drinking makes me emotional," Jesse said with a small smile.

Zach smiled back. "Something tells me you would be emotional telling this story even without the wine."

"I know what you're thinking. How could someone who couldn't afford to keep a horse she loved afford to buy all this?"

She made a half circle with her arm.

Zach didn't say anything.

The bottle of wine was almost empty and Jesse was way past her limit. She leaned forward, motioning him closer with her finger. When Zach leaned toward her, she pressed her lips to his. He tasted sweet and his mouth was warm from the wine.

"Sorry. I've wanted to do that since you got here," Jesse said, licking her lips. "Would you like to know where I get my money?" Jesse asked mischievously.

"Only if you'd like to tell me."

It wasn't that Jesse didn't want people to know she'd won the lottery, it just wasn't something she advertised.

Leaning in closer to Zach like she had the biggest secret in the world, she whispered, "I won the lottery."

"Really?"

"Really and truly. I cashed in my ticket, gave half to my ex, said goodbye to him and his car, and here I am." Jesse sat back and smiled. She felt she could trust Zach to not to tell anyone about her money. She also felt she could trust him not to take advantage because she had money. How did she know this? She wasn't sure, but she did.

"Now you have to tell me about you."

"That's a story for another night," Zach replied, getting up. Jesse followed him into the house and hopped up on the counter next to the sink.

"That's not fair. Just tell me a little something."

Zach set the mugs in the sink and turned to her, leaning his hip against the counter. "There's not much to tell."

Jesse didn't believe him. "Okay, then just give me the quick version of what went on with you and Sally. And you can't say nothing happened. She looked like she wanted to spray you with whip cream and devour you the other night."

Zach stood in front of her and positioned himself between her legs. Smiling, he gave her a light kiss.

"We dated briefly after high school. Sally was possessive and wanted to settle down. I didn't. I was going off to college.

I wasn't ready for a wife and kids, so I broke it off before I left. She's tried to get me to hook up with her ever since."

"Did you sleep with her?" Jesse asked before she could stop herself.

"No, I didn't sleep with her. Back then I was a respectable boy." He leaned toward her, his lips barely touching hers.

Jesse licked her lips. "And now?" Jesse asked as she ran a finger along the waistband of his jeans

"Not so much," he said, allowing their lips to meet more firmly.

Jesse was feeling more than a little excited from drinking the wine and couldn't wait to get her hands on Zach. Wrapping her arms and legs around him, the kiss quickly went from soft to demanding.

Pulling him to her, she ran her hands up the back of his shirt. The heat from his skin seemed to soak into her hands and flow through her. He was hot and hard—and she wanted him.

To feel this way when a man touched her ... She arched her back when Zach kissed her neck. His breath was hot on her skin as he trailed kisses over the tops of her breasts. Pulling the V of her shirt down, he exposed her breasts and placed his mouth on a nipple.

Jesse moaned as she ran her hands through his hair. Her hands traveled to his zipper when Zach broke away, leaving her staring at him.

"I should go," he said, stepping back.

"Now?" Jesse exclaimed. She jumped off the counter suddenly sobered and stood in front of him with her hands on her hips. "You're going to leave me like this?" She'd made up her mind about him. She wanted him.

Zach looked her over as if he couldn't believe what he was about to do.

"Unfortunately, yes. You drank a lot and I wouldn't feel right."

Jesse was shocked. She had finally found a man who turned

her on beyond her wildest dreams and he had to go and have morals.

Zach turned to leave. "Don't forget to lock up," he said as he walked to the door.

Jesse followed him out. "I thought you weren't respectable anymore," she yelled after him.

Zach smiled and got into the truck. Leaving was hard, but when he and Jesse got together they would both be fully aware of what they were doing.

# Chapter Eleven

*J*esse was busy the next few days getting the house in order. The rest of her belongings had arrived the day before. She'd worked all day to get everything put away and now she had nothing to do. She thought about going shopping but really didn't feel like it.

She'd made several trips to Butte. Besides hitting the local Home Depot and Wal-Mart, she found a wholesale store where she stocked up on several items.

Since she was in no hurry, Jesse would take detours during her shopping trips. The history in Montana was unbelievable. From Lewis and Clark to Indians and gold diggers. Montana was the real west.

There were several museums and national parks she wanted to see, but would wait to see them with Emma. Although she'd done research before moving, Jesse picked up a few books on the area. She'd started to see some wildlife around the ranch and wanted to be familiar with what might be dangerous.

Her favorite time of day was morning. She'd take her coffee out on the deck, and if she sat quietly, usually saw some deer. Jesse had yet to see any moose and thankfully no bears had come near the house, at least not that she knew of. In the evenings she could hear coyotes in the distance.

She'd have to have part of the yard fenced before her dogs arrived from Connecticut next week. She'd also feel better about letting Emma play outside if there was a contained area where no wild animals could come in.

Sitting out on the deck, Jesse thought of Zach. She had enjoyed his company the other night, and his kisses even more. Although a little afraid of the intensity of her attraction to him, she was also very curious about it. Every time she saw him it was the same. Instant heat flowed through her.

Jesse smiled. She'd become a very wanton woman. Climbing on him in the furniture store had been liberating. She had felt like a seductive vixen. She'd felt like a woman.

Grabbing her keys, she headed out the door. He did agree to let her come and work at the ranch. Why not today?

•

Jesse parked her truck and got out. It was quiet and she didn't see anyone. Walking into the barn she saw Ty in the wash stall standing patiently.

"What are you doing out here by yourself?" she asked, walking up to pet him.

"Can I help you?"

Jesse jumped back. She wasn't expecting anyone to come walking out from behind the horse.

The man stepped around Ty. He looked to be in his early twenties. Brown hair cut short and soft brown eyes. He was maybe six foot and in very good shape. His arms were tan and toned. *What a cutie.*

"Um, I'm looking for Zach," Jesse answered looking around at the tools on the floor. "You're the horse shoe guy?"

"Yeah. I'm Josh," he said, dimples showing as he smiled.

"Nice to meet you. I'm Jesse. I just bought the ranch next door."

Josh bent over to pick up a tool and work on Ty's hoof.

*Why are they all so young,* she thought. *I don't remember guys looking like this when I was twenty.*

Deep in thought and staring at Josh's backside, Jesse didn't notice Zach standing in the doorway. Not caring that she had been caught checking Josh out, she gave Zach a smirk and shrugged her shoulders. What could she say? The boy was nice to look at.

"Hey, Zach," Josh said. "I'm about done here. Any other horses you need done?"

Zach pushed away from the doorway and walked over to where they were standing. "Not today. I have to go back out. Just leave the bill on the desk."

"You got it," Josh said as he went back to work.

Zach turned his eyes to Jesse. "Jesse," he said so smoothly that it forced Jesse to look at him. "Was I supposed to meet you today?"

Jesse put her hands in her back pockets. "Nope. Just thought I'd come over and help. Remember you said I could do some things around here?"

Star was tied to a post and he walked over to her. "I have to ride back out and fix a downed fence. I came back for some tools. Do you want to ride out with me?"

"Can I use the hammer?" she asked, rocking back on her heels.

"If you promise not to break my fingers," he said, swinging up into the saddle and holding out his hand to her.

"How about I wait for Ty to be done and follow later?"

Zach just looked at her with eyes that said "no way."

"Fine," she said, taking his hand to swing up behind him.

"You should at least let me sit in the saddle," she said. "I am a guest."

"Guest? I thought you came to work?"

"I did. I'm a working guest," she said, wrapping her arms around his midsection as they started to ride off.

Jesse could feel Zach's muscles through his shirt. She wanted to run her hands up his chest and feel the rest of him. She sighed. Maybe riding in the back wasn't so bad.

"Hold on," Zach said as he nudged Star into a canter.

Having a good hold on Zach, Jesse leaned back some and lifted her face upward. The wind blew her hair and caressed her face. The sun was warm on her skin. She'd never felt so free, so alive. Jesse felt like she was flying. Her whole body relaxed and moved with the motion of the horse.

Putting his hand on top of hers to hold her where she was, Zach nudged Star faster.

She pulled herself back up against Zach and took a deep breath. He smelled so masculine. She loved the scent of him. He was so opposite what Paul had been. Zach's jeans were worn and comfortable looking. His shirts soft to the touch. His hair uncombed. His face rough with stubble.

She loved comfortable, loved casual. Jeans, sneakers, boots, T-shirts, flannel pajamas on a cold night ... The man in front of her was exactly what she craved. What she needed and wanted.

Jesse felt Star slow to a walk and peeked around Zach to see where they were. She saw a fence in front of them that had some downed rails. There were no horses around and she wondered what this area was used for.

"We use it for fall grazing," Zach answered when she asked. "Before the winter comes, we'll take the horses up here to graze for a month or so. It's the last grass they have for awhile."

When Zach picked up one of the boards, Jesse walked over with the hammer.

He watched her carelessly swing the hammer. "Promise you'll hit the nail?" he asked.

"Now Zach," she said sweetly, walking over to place a nail onto the board, "do you really think I want to damage those beautiful hands? If I did then you wouldn't be able to run them all over my body."

Zach opened his mouth to say something then stopped.

Finishing up with the first board they moved onto the others.

"So, do you think Josh will still be there when we get back? I should have him over to talk about what my horses' shoeing needs will be."

"Since you don't have any horses yet how can you discuss their needs?" He held the next board in place.

"Well, I have a general idea what needs to be done. I should really make sure he's qualified first." Jesse looked up at him and grinned.

She was teasing him and he knew it. He looked like he actually enjoyed it. "Kind of like when you offered me a job and I had to show you I'd be qualified?"

Jesse hit the last nail and straightened. "Exactly. Any more?" She hit the nail one last time.

"Nope. That's it." Zach walked over to Star and placed the tools back in the saddlebag. "Ready to go?"

"Sure." She watched as he swung his leg over the saddle and settled in. She took the hand he held out and swung up behind him, a mischievous grin playing on her face.

Zach turned Star in the direction of home and started off. He was not unaware of Jesse pressed against his back. On the contrary, he was very aware. Maybe too aware of how she felt against him.

Sitting with her arms wrapped around him, she couldn't help but touch him. She started slow. Opening her fingers, spreading them across his stomach. She smiled as she felt the muscles tighten under her touch.

Moving her hand to the waistband of his pants, she grabbed his shirt and slowly pulled it from his jeans. Feeling the end of the shirt leave his pants, she moved her hands under to touch his skin.

She moved her hands across his rib cage, making her way up his chest. His skin was smooth and warm. His muscles tight. She stopped to play with the bit of hair that spread across his chest. Running her hands through it, she circled his nipples lightly with her fingertips. Jesse wanted to touch him until she died.

Zach sucked in his breath at the touch of her hands on his skin. "Jesse?"

"Yes?"

"What are you doing?" His voice was as tight as his muscles.

"What does it look like I'm doing?" she asked. "I'm feeling you up."

Zach stopped the horse but didn't remove her hands.

"I was bored back here and can't see around you." Jesse was trying to sound as innocent as she could. "Maybe if you let me sit in the front—"

"Jesse," he said, taking a deep breath as she ran her hand across the other nipple. "I can't let you sit in front of me."

"That's not fair. How about we just try it?" she said.

Before he could answer, she swung her leg up and hooked it around him. Then holding onto him, maneuvered around so she was not so much sitting in front of him as on him.

Zach didn't breathe. She'd swung around him and was now sitting on his lap facing him with her legs locked around his waist and her arms around his neck.

"There now, isn't this better?"

Zach groaned and nudged Star back into a walk.

Jesse knew she was hurting Zach, but not in a bad way. She could feel his hardness through his pants. If he asked her to move back behind him, she would.

Zach looked straight ahead as he tried to regain control over his body. Her hands continued to run over his chest and although he tried to focus on the trees in the distance, he was losing the battle.

Jesse unbuttoned Zach's shirt and admired what she saw. His chest muscles were perfect. Not an ounce of fat fell over the waist of his jeans.

Taking a quick glance at his face, she smiled and leaned forward to run her tongue around a nipple. She could feel the muscles twitching as she placed light kisses on him.

When she looked back up at him, he was staring down at her. Jesse had not seduced many men, but she knew she had Zach right where she wanted him. She could see the want she felt mirrored in his eyes.

With her eyes never leaving his, she took his free hand and moved it under her shirt to her breast. She bit her lower lip as she moved it in a circular motion over her breast.

The roughness of his hands against the smoothness of her

breast was driving her wild. Jesse arched back as Zach took over. Her chest rose in heavy breaths. Once she took his hand, there had been no going back.

Jesse felt air hit her skin and closed her eyes. Her breath caught when his tongue circle around a nipple. She moaned when he took it into his mouth. Running one hand through his hair, she pulled him closer, forcing him to become rougher with her.

Lifting his head, Zach captured her lips. Jesse wrapped her arms around his neck pulling her body against his.

Through her own jeans, she could feel Zach pulsing between her legs. As she rubbed against him, she could feel the climax building. She wasn't sure he would be able to get there, too, but if he didn't, she would willingly allow him to strip her naked and take her right there.

Jesse stopped kissing Zach and clung to him as she moved against him. He couldn't move, so she had to. She felt his arms tighten around her, pushing her harder against him.

The feeling that was building inside her was one she had never felt. It was so big, so strong, that when she came she bit Zach's shoulder to keep from crying out.

Zach tensed when Jesse did. He let himself go.

Jesse rested her head on Zach's shoulder as they tried to catch their breath. Both of them knew whether they wanted to admit it or not, things between them had just changed.

# Chapter Twelve

$A$lthough she loved the solitude of her ranch, Jesse loved the town of Dillon. Since the weather was good she'd often go into town and grab a sandwich from the diner then head over to the park.

Sitting on the park bench she was able to meet a few mothers with their kids. Most were friendly and would stop to say hello and introduce themselves. They would share stories of the towns inhabitants, often making Jesse laugh.

The people of Dillon loved their town and their neighbors. Jesse felt blessed that they were welcoming her so easily.

"Hi."

Jesse looked up from her paper to see a face she recognized, but didn't know. It was Zach's friend who had stopped him outside the diner the night Zach had come to Jesse's hotel room.

"I'm Jimmy," he said, holding out his hand. "We didn't get a chance to meet the night you were with Zach."

Jesse smiled and took his hand. "Nice to meet you, Jimmy. I'm Jesse. I moved in down the road from Zach."

"Yeah, I know," he said shyly as he sat down.

He looked to be a few years younger than Jesse. Very cute in a boy-next-door kind of way. His blond hair was wavy and he had blue eyes. Not dark like Zach's, but a lighter sky blue.

"How do you like Dillon?" he asked.

"It's really wonderful here. I love the small town feel. Everyone has been so nice. I feel like I fit in already."

Jesse could tell he was a little nervous. Maybe he didn't have a lot of experience talking to girls.

"Have you always lived here?" Jesse asked.

"Since I was ten. We lived in Billings before. Since the rodeo is coming back next week, the town has a big picnic before. Do you think you'll be going? I'd be happy to go with you if so you won't have to go alone."

Jesse was flattered, but didn't want to give him the impression she was interested.

"Well, I—"

"She won't be alone."

Jesse looked past Jimmy to see Zach a few feet away. Where he'd come from, she wasn't sure.

"How's it going, Jimmy? Jesse," he said with a nod to her.

"It's going okay." Jimmy looked to Jesse then back at Zach. He knew when to back off. "I guess I'll get going. It was nice talking to you."

"You, too."

Zach took the spot on the bench that Jimmy had vacated so quickly.

"I think you scared him," Jesse said.

"Me? It was probably you. He's always had a hard time around girls. I'm surprised he asked you to go to the picnic with him." He took bite of the apple he'd been carrying.

"I might have said yes since I didn't know I already had a date," she said. "Who is it?"

Zach grinned at her, as if even with her hair in a ponytail and jogging pants on, he thought she looked beautiful. He leaned forward and kissed her softly.

"Is it someone I know?" she asked when their lips separated.

"You're funny, you know that?" he said, taking another bite of the apple. "I'll pick you up about one." He got up to leave.

"I haven't said yes."

"Darlin, one thing I do know is that you can't say no to me." Zach winked at her as he turned and walked out of the park.

Jesse smiled as she watched him go. He was right.

•

"Are you sure it's okay to leave her alone?" Jesse asked. They were on their way to the picnic, but Jesse was concerned about Zach's pregnant mare who was ready to foal any day.

"She'll be fine. I have Bob stopping in to check on her. He'll call if anything happens."

Jesse wasn't convinced it was okay, but Zach had more experience in this area than she did. She looked out the window and enjoyed the ride. She'd met quite a few people in her wanderings around the town, but today she'd get to meet everyone, including Zach's family.

He told her his mother and sister always came over for the picnic. Not that she was nervous or anything. It's not like she and Zach were a couple, and there was no reason his family shouldn't like her.

*Admit it Jesse, you're nervous about meeting his mother. So what if all you want to do is jump his bones. It's not like it's written on your face and everyone at the picnic will know.*

Jesse glanced over at him. He had on her favorite pair of faded jeans with a dark blue T-shirt. Instead of boots he wore sneakers. Today he looked more jock than cowboy.

The picnic was held at the park. Streets were blocked off and there were vendors set up selling goods. Parents let their kids run free while they set up in their chosen spot.

Walking toward the center of the park, Zach headed for a large oak tree. There were already a few blankets spread in the area and Jesse could see two women putting out food.

One of the women stopped and watched as they approached. Jesse felt Zach take her hand.

"You okay?" he asked.

"Promise you won't leave me until they're done drilling me with questions?"

Zach laughed. "They're really not that bad. Be prepared to give them a wedding date, though."

Jesse's mouth opened but nothing came out. Feeling slightly

ill all of the sudden, she wondered if she should have accepted Jimmy's invitation.

"Zach." The older women hugged him. "You must be Jesse," she said, turning her attention to Jesse. "We're glad you were able to join us."

"Jesse, this is my mother, Amanda Baker."

"It's a pleasure to meet you," Jesse said. Jesse could see Zach in his mother. Her eyes were the same color, and her smile was the same as Zach's. She was short, like Jesse, which probably meant Zach's father had been tall.

"And this," Zach said, hugging the other women who had walked up, "is my baby sister, Kellie."

Kellie offered her hand to Jesse. "He only calls me that because he knows I hate being called the baby."

Kellie didn't quite have Zach's height, but she was taller than Jesse. She was slim and fit. Her straight brown hair hung down to the middle of her back.

"Uncle Zach." Jesse turned to see Zach scoop up a little girl. She looked to be six or seven, and squealed with delight as Zach swung her around.

"Katie," he said, walking over to Jesse, "this is my friend, Jesse."

The little girl eyed Jesse suspiciously, obviously concerned that Jesse was butting in on her territory.

"It's very nice to meet you, Katie," Jesse said. "I have a little girl about your age. She'll be here in a few weeks. Maybe you can come over once she gets here."

"Maybe."

"Don't worry about that one," Kellie said to Jesse as Zach went to play Frisbee with Katie. "Zach is her favorite. He spoils her rotten."

Jesse helped spread the other blankets and set the food out. "Is Reese coming? I haven't met him yet."

"No. He's with Alex at the rodeo. When Alex rides, Reese tries to go whenever he can. They'll be back next week when the rodeo is here."

Jesse watched Zach play with Katie. He was good with her. She could see the smile on his face and it made her smile. She missed Emma and wished she could be there; it would have been good for her to meet other kids.

"He's good with kids. Always has been." Amanda had walked up to stand beside Jesse. "How old is your daughter?"

Jesse smiled as she watched Zach purposely miss the Frisbee. "She's seven."

"She'll get along fine here. The kids are friendly and there are lots of activities. Get her involved and she'll feel right at home."

Jesse smiled at the older women, already liking her.

"Jesse, this is my husband, Peter, and my son, Michael."

Jesse turned to Kellie and saw a handsome dark haired man and boy with her. Peter had the friendliest smile Jesse had ever seen. Dimples shown on either side of his mouth and the smile touched his brown eyes. Michael was a smaller version of his father. Dressed in a baseball uniform that was smudged with dirt, his smile was just as friendly.

"It's a pleasure to meet both of you."

"Mom, can I go and see if Jeff and Kyle are here yet?" Michael asked, grabbing a handful of chips.

"Get changed first. I brought extra clothes for you in the car."

"Thanks, Mom." With a kiss to his mother's cheek, Michael took off.

"So how do you like Montana so far?" Peter asked as he sat on the picnic bench.

"So far I love it," Jesse said. She glanced at Zach. "I really like the quiet of the area, but also that there are larger cities close by."

Peter didn't miss Jesse's glace in Zach's direction. "Wait until the winter comes. You might change your mind."

Jesse smiled. "Maybe. But honestly, I'm looking forward to it. It can't be that bad. We get pretty cold winters back east."

Peter shook his head. "Not like here."

"Not like here what?" Zach asked as he came up behind Jesse and hugged her.

"I was just filling Jesse in on the winters here. Winter in Montana makes the ones back east seem like spring time."

Zach sat down next to Peter and leaned back against the table. "Jesse's pretty resourceful," Zach said with a grin. "I'm sure she'll find some way to keep warm."

"Well," Jesse said smiling. "I've already ordered my flannel sheets and down comforter. L.L. Bean will be making a fortune off me this year."

"Honey, you're going to need more than long underwear under those flannel sheets," Zach said.

Jesse looked over at Peter, giving him a half grin then stepped in front of Zach. Leaning down she brought her face close to his.

"Honey," she said, looking into his blue eyes, "I never mentioned underwear of any sort, and who said that's all I'd have under the sheets?"

Turning, she walked off.

"Any idea what she was talking about?" Peter asked as he watched Jesse walk away.

•

Jesse leaned back against Zach and sighed. She didn't want this day to end. It was the most fun she'd had in a long time. The food and company had been wonderful. Jesse really liked Zach's family. She could see how much they loved and enjoyed each other.

Zach tormented Kellie by telling stories of when she was in junior high school and chasing boys. But Kellie retaliated by letting out tales of how Zach and Hunter had to make a run for it in their underwear several times from fathers with shotguns.

Zach's family welcomed her with no questions asked. They treated her like she and Zach had been together for years. Jesse stopped mid-thought. Were she and Zach together? She really wasn't sure. They'd spent a lot of time together the past week, and today he acted like they were a couple. Jesse didn't want to assume too much. She really wasn't sure she was ready to be half of anything.

Zach hugged her back against him. *No need to worry about stuff like that now.*

Jess felt Zach's phone vibrate as they watched the fireworks explode above.

"How far along? Okay, I'm on my way."

Jesse turned to face Zach. "The mare?"

"Yeah. I'll drop you at home on my way."

Jesse stood. "No. I want to come with you."

"Are you sure? It could be a long night."

Jesse shook her head and started to pick up the blanket while Zach said quick goodbyes to everyone.

When Zach and Jesse reached the barn the mare was pacing nervously around. She'd stop and lift her hind leg, kicking at her stomach every few steps. Having given birth herself, Jesse knew how the mare must feel.

"How long will it take?" Jesse asked as she watched the mare drink some water.

Zach had stepped into the stall to examine the mare. "Could be hours. But she's pretty far along. We just have to wait."

Coming out of the stall, Zach went into the office to put a pot of coffee on. The vet had been out only a few days ago and confirmed the foal was in the proper position to birth. So Zach didn't anticipate any complications.

Zach handed Jesse a mug and sat down on the floor outside the stall.

"Is there anything we should get for her?" Jesse asked sitting beside him.

"No. She knows what to do. This is her second. She's been through this before."

Jesse smiled. She thought back to the night Emma was born. She didn't even know she was in labor until the pain was so bad.

She looked over at Zach. His head was back against the wall

and his eyes were closed. When he opened them and looked at her, she was sure she felt her heart melt.

"Do you want kids?"

"I do someday. How about you? Is Emma enough for you?"

"No. I always wanted her to have a sibling. I felt guilty that she would grow up alone, but I also knew having another child with Paul wasn't the right thing to do. It wouldn't save our marriage."

Jesse looked at him and knew he'd make a great father. He was caring, affectionate, had a great work ethic and family was important to him. She knew he would always make time for his kids.

"Besides, it wouldn't have been fair to the child. I love being a mom. Emma is my life. I have no problem giving up my free time to spend it with her." Jesse looked down into her mug. "I just didn't think I'd be happy having another child. The extra work to take care of a baby." She looked over at him. "I know it sounds selfish, but I just didn't want to be a bad mom because I was overwhelmed."

Zach said he didn't think that was selfish, but smart. There were so many people in the world who had children who shouldn't. The fact she thought of how she would affect a child's life made her a great mom.

Hearing a whinny and rustling of hay, Zach got up and went into the stall. The mare was laying on her side and Jesse could see the tip of a hoof starting to come out.

Not sure what to do, she went over and knelt by the mare's head. She spoke to her is soft tones hoping that would give the horse comfort.

Zach stayed by her hind end, not too close, but where he could get to her quickly if she needed any help.

Jesse watched in awe as a small head and hooves appeared, followed by a chest and torso. The foal just seemed to slide out effortlessly.

It was covered with mucus, which Zach gently wiped away

with towels. The mare lifted her head, looked at her baby, then laid her head back down.

Zach looked over at Jesse smiling. "Amazing, isn't it?"

Jesse stood and stepped back as the mare stood and walked over to her baby. She watched as the mama horse began to clean the foal. It was the most amazing thing Jesse had ever witnessed.

Jesse rested her head against Zach's arm. She didn't realize how tired she was until just then.

Zach looked down at her. "Why don't you go up to the house and change? There should be something in my closet you can throw on. I have to push fresh straw down, then I'll be up."

Jesse looked down at herself. She was covered in dirt, and wet from where the mare's head had been resting on her lap. With each step she felt more tired. Her watch read just after 2:00 AM.

Reaching his closet, she put on a pair of Zach's shorts and a T-shirt. After washing her face she felt much better. She thought she'd just lie on the couch for a minute until Zach got back, then he could take her home.

•

Zach finished spreading the straw and checked to make sure all the horses had enough water before going up to the house. What a day. He had a great time at the picnic with Jesse. His mother and sister had even behaved themselves and didn't grill him about her.

The fact his niece had shared a cookie with her after lunch was a huge indication that Jesse was special. Zach smiled.

Yes she was special. He really liked Jesse, and with each day that passed he became more comfortable with the growing attraction he had to her.

Locking the back door he turned to go down the hall and saw her. She was sound asleep on the couch. She had on a pair of his old running shorts and a worn Yankees shirt.

Man did she look sexy in his clothes. *I bet she looks even better out of them.*

Walking over to her he grabbed the blanket off the back of the couch. Spreading it across her he gave her a soft kiss on her temple.

He smiled when she gave a little sigh.

Leaving a table light on in case she woke up, he went down the hall to take a shower.

•

Jesse opened her eyes and had to think for a second where she was. Zach's. The picnic. The mare. She could hear water running and went down the hall to the bedroom.

The bathroom door was cracked open a bit and she looked in. Jesse's blood raced when she saw Zach in the shower. Although she knew she should, she couldn't look away. She was so captured by him. She watched as he soaped his chest and arms, then turned toward the water to rinse. His tanned skin glistened.

Jesse felt the tingling between her legs grow when Zach stepped out of the shower and she saw his full body. He was magnificent. His arms and legs toned and tight. Jesse watched as he dried himself, all the while envisioning his hands running over her skin.

Zach wrapped the towel around himself and looked up to find Jesse in the doorway staring at him. He wasn't ashamed, just surprised.

He could see her chest rising in heavy breaths. Her eyes were devouring him and he could feel himself hardening under the towel.

Jesse walked over to stand in front of him. She could feel the heat on his skin from the shower. She looked him over from head to feet, pausing where the towel had risen some.

She lightly ran her hand over his shoulders and down his chest. She brushed his nipple and saw his muscle twitch. Her hands went lower, tracing his abdominal muscles and stopped where the towel rested on his hips.

Jesse looked up into his eyes. "I want you, Zach."

Zach paused, searching her face. He couldn't find any reason not to be with Jesse. His hands came up to cup her face. Running a thumb along her lower lip, he bent to kiss her.

Zach kissed her with a gentleness and passion that made her knees grow weak. Feeling herself being lifted, she wrapped her arms around his neck.

Carrying her to his bed, Zach was overwhelmed with his want for Jesse. The kissing, the teasing, the insinuating words, had all led to this.

Laying her down, Zach stepped back and removed the towel. He let her eyes roam over him before lying next to her. The moon shown through the windows providing just enough light to see each other. Jesse laid back and allowed Zach to remove her clothes until she was as naked as him.

She ached for him to touch her and was rewarded a moment later when he lay next to her and ran a hand over her stomach. She had never been touched in such a way. He was caressing her body, and although she was crazy with desire for him, she was loving every minute it took.

Zach ran a hand over each breast, running his palm over her nipples until they were hard. He savored the feel of Jesse's skin. She was soft and smooth. His hand followed the curve of her hip, down her side to her thigh where he brought it across and settled it between her legs.

Lifting her hips, Jesse pressed against his hand and opened her legs. She rubbed against him, closing her eyes to the exquisite feelings building inside her.

She caught her breath when she felt a finger slide in, then another. He seemed to know exactly what to do, where to touch.

Opening her eyes, Jesse looked into Zach's. It was time. She could come this way, but didn't want to. She wanted him inside her. She wanted to feel all of him.

Putting her hand behind his neck, she pulled him toward her for a demanding kiss. She wrapped a hand around him and gently pulled, stoking him until he, too, became just as demanding.

The kiss broke and Jesse felt him reaching over her to the night stand drawer and pulling out a condom. Then he was above her, lowering his hips down to her.

Jesse held her breath. The anticipation she was feeling was so great. She wanted to grab Zach's hips and pull him down to her. She felt him stop and rest the tip of himself against her.

As he kissed her, he let the rest of himself slide in. The feel of him fully inside her was incredible. He filled her so completely that she knew Zach would be a lover like she'd never had.

Moving with him, she gave in as wave after wave of desire flooded her. She could feel the blood coursing through her. She wanted what was building in her to be released, and at the same time, wanted it never to end.

She couldn't think. Could only feel so many things. The wanting, the desire—it was all there in her just waiting to get out.

Jesse moaned, her body shuddering its release as Zach tensed above her. She savored the feel of Zach's body on hers as she regained her senses. *That is what sex was supposed to be like*, Jesse thought.

Planting a kiss on her lips, Zach rolled off her and went into the bathroom. "Hey," Jesse said frowning.

When Zach came back out her eyes narrowed as she looked at him. A feeling she had never experienced came over her. She already wanted him again.

"Zaaach," Jesse purred as she pulled back the sheets for him.

Zach watched her. The look on her face went from sedated and satisfied, to hot and wanting in a matter of seconds. The sex they just had was some of the best he had ever experienced.

He could definitely get used to this. What a way to unwind after a long day, he thought as he climbed back under the sheets.

# Chapter Thirteen

*J*esse was excited about having a girl's day out. Although much younger than Jesse, she and Jen shared similar interests. *The Baker boys being one,* Jesse thought.

Jesse sipped her coffee as she waited for Jen's shift to end. Hearing the bell on the door she looked up to see Hunter come in.

"Mind if I join you?" he asked.

"Not at all," Jesse replied. Jen just looked at Jesse with raised eyebrows, and after taking an order from Hunter, walked away.

"I was hoping to see you," he said, sliding rodeo tickets across the table. "I brought these so you'd have no choice but to come and see me next week."

Jesse thanked him; it was kind of him to think of her and she was really excited about the rodeo.

"How's the ranch coming along?" Hunter asked, taking a sip of coffee.

Jesse told him of her numerous trips to the store and never-ending lists of things she thought she'd need.

The bell jingled again. Turning to look, Hunter saw Zach glance at them and walk over to the counter.

Jesse's brow knit together. Why didn't Zach didn't come over? After the night they spent together, she'd been unable to get Zach out of her mind, not that she was able to stop thinking about him before that. What had happened was just a glimpse of what they both could expect. Jesse felt warm just thinking about it.

When Zach started to leave without so much as an acknowledgement that Jesse was there, she excused herself and intercepted him at the door.

"Weren't you even going to say hello?" Jesse asked looking up at him.

She didn't know why he had such a hard look on his face, but when he looked down at her, his eyes were dark. Was he regretting what had happened between them?

"Do you think you can come by the ranch? I wanted to ask you some things about the old barn," Jesse asked.

Zach wasn't even looking at her, never mind paying attention to what she was saying. She looked back over her shoulder to see what did have his attention and saw he was watching Hunter talked to Jen.

Jen was laughing about something Hunter had said. Surely he didn't think Jen was interested in Hunter? First he was too old for her, and second, it was obvious how much she loved Jeremy.

"I wouldn't get too attached to Hunter if I were you," Zach said ,still looking at Hunter.

Jesse looked over her shoulder. Why would did Zach think she would get attached to Hunter? Surely her having breakfast with him would not upset Zach. Would it? Was Zach jealous? Jesse smiled.

"So do you think you can come by? If not I can ask Hunter. He seems pretty knowledgeable and could probably help me out." *I'm so evil*.

Zach's jaw twitched and he looked down at her slowly. "I'll be by later," he said and turned to leave.

"Not too early. I'll be out most of the afternoon."

Zach stopped mid-stride as if he was going to say something, but then continued out the door. Jesse turned to and tried not to laugh. She was right. He was jealous.

•

Zach left the diner and drove over to his grandfather's

store. He'd gone to the diner hoping to catch Jesse there and have breakfast with her. It had caught him off guard when he walked in and saw her sitting with Hunter.

It's not that he didn't like Hunter. They had been good friends growing up and had just drifted apart as they got older. Zach had gone off to college and Hunter went on the rodeo circuit. Zach knew Jesse was aware of Hunter's reputation with women, yet she still seemed to like him—and that bothered Zach.

Jealousy gnawing at him. He went into the feed store. He looked around trying to remember what he had come to town for in the first place.

"Morning, Zach," Bill said.

"Morning," Zach said grumpily.

"What can I get for you?"

"I need more of that hoof supplement and oil. One of the colts is still having problems with cracked hooves." Zach went and got what he needed and went to the counter. "Didn't  you say Jesse met Hunter here last week?"

"Sure did. He actually helped her pick out some things. They seemed to get along fine. Why?" Bill asked.

Zach told his grandfather about seeing Jesse with Hunter this morning. "Jesse's a smart girl. She can take care of herself. But—" Bill started then stopped.

Zach glared at him. "What?"

"Well, Hunter did say he would be riding in the rodeo and Jesse seemed pretty interested in going."

Bill chuckled as Zach left the store.

•

Shopping with Jen turned out to be an adventure.

Jen made her try on clothes that were definitely not for her. They had laughed so hard Jesse's sides hurt.

"So, what's going on with you and Zach?" Jen asked.

Jesse wanted to spill the beans, but didn't think she should share her newfound sex life with her almost as-new-friend. But she could give hints. Jen was smart; she'd figure it out.

"What do you mean? Zach's helping me with the ranch," Jesse said, sipping her drink.

"He's helping you with more than the ranch, I think. Whenever you talk about him, you try not to talk about him," Jen said. "Zach is a major catch. There are at least twenty women in three counties who would love to bag him."

Jesse just smiled and remembered. "Well, I don't want to bag him." *I just want him naked and in bed.*

"Well, everyone's talking about you two."

"Why?" Jesse asked, knitting her eyebrows together.

"Why? Because Zach never takes his dates where anyone will see him, never mind the town picnic."

Jen paused to take a drink.

"Zach hasn't had a steady girlfriend in over ten years. Ever since he came back to Dillon and bought his ranch. He pretty much stays to himself. He's a guy, so I assume he dates some. But never anything steady."

Jesse wasn't sure what to make of this information.

"Well, Zach and I are just friends."

"But you do like him?" Jen asked.

Jesse could have laughed at that one. "Yeah, I would say I like him."

"Good. With Zach as the focus, maybe everyone will get off Jeremy and me about getting married."

"Wait a second, don't go marrying us off yet."

"Oh, I won't," Jen paused and smiled. "Yet."

# Chapter Fourteen

*J*esse got changed and went down to the kitchen to make something to eat. She wondered if Zach would come by like he said he would. Hopefully he wasn't still mad at seeing her with Hunter.

Jesse liked Hunter but he wasn't her type. The few times they'd meet he'd been nice, but there was no way she'd be able to deal with a big ego or rodeo groupies chasing him around. *Been there, done that.*

When she heard a car door, she smiled and stepped onto the deck. "Hey there cowboy."

"Have a good afternoon?" he asked grumpily.

*He's angry with me!* "It was fantastic. I had the best time," Jesse said leaning on the deck rail, a dreamy look on her face. She knew she was being horrible by teasing him, but she couldn't help it. She came down the stairs. "Ready to look at the barn?" She walked by him.

Looking over her shoulder at him, she smiled sweetly.

Zach took a deep breath and followed her. When they reached the barn she asked several questions about how to repair the barn and update it. He was only half listening and told her he'd have to get back to her on some things.

As they walked back to the house Jesse asked, "Do you want to go to the rodeo with me next week? Hunter gave me some tickets."

Zach looked at her suspiciously. "I'm not really the rodeo type."

"That's okay. I don't mind going alone. If you can't make it Hunter told me I could stay with him." Jesse watched his face and continued, "I can't wait to see the broncs and bulls. Actually it might be better if I go alone."

Zach's eyes narrowed.

"Are you okay?" Jesse asked trying not to smile. "You look a bit flushed."

It took him all of two seconds to come and stand on the stair just below her so that they were face to face. "Stay away from Hunter," he said a scowl on his face.

Jesse could see his jaw twitch. Crossing her arms on her chest, she asked, "And why would I want to do that?"

Zach looked at her. His eyes were the darkest blue she'd ever seen, a dark and dangerous blue that made Jesse's blood race.

"Just stay away from him, Jesse."

Standing tall, Jesse smirked at him. "Make me," she replied.

He was on her in a heartbeat. He was kissing her like he was a dying man and she was his last meal. His hands roamed her body, feeling every inch before settling on her backside and pulling her against him.

She wrapped her arms around him and kissed him back with everything she had. Her breathing became ragged. She couldn't get enough of him.

This was different from the other night. This was a new experience. There was no waiting, no foreplay.

Jesse broke the kiss and jumped up to wrap her legs around his waist and then planted her mouth back on his.

Zach had no choice but to hold her up. He took a step up and backed her into the wall of the house. Having her against something solid allowed Zach to press his body against hers. The pants Jesse had on were thin and she could feel him against her. Jesse moaned and it was instinct to grind her hips against him.

Zach made a noise low in his throat and moved away from

the wall into the house. For him the bedroom was just too far.

He lowered himself to the floor, on that rug, with Jesse still wrapped around him. When her back hit the floor he removed his mouth from hers to pull her shirt off.

Taking her breast in his hand he roughly ran a thumb over the nipple. Jesse arched up to him. When he took a nipple between his teeth she whimpered as he teased.

She lifted her hips, allowing her pants to be removed, all while savoring the feel of both the slickness of his tongue and the roughness of his face on her breasts.

Jesse grabbed at his shirt, forcing him to break contact with her breast as she pulled it over his head. She ran her hands over his chest and down to the waistband of his pants.

With her fingers on the buttons, she paused and looked up at him. His eyes bore into her, heating her within.

Zach watched as she unbuttoned his pants. Undoing the zipper she ran her hand into his jeans. When she took him in her hand, he closed his eyes and drew in his breath.

He was big in her hands, and Jesse wanted him inside her now.

"Please tell me you brought something."

Zach stood and reached into his pocket, producing a wallet and a condom. He stripped himself of his jeans before settling on top of her.

When Zach's skin finally came into contact with hers, Jesse thought she would explode right then. The passion and desire made her feel as if she were going crazy.

She could feel him pressing between her legs, the tip of him just entering her. Running her fingers through his hair, she pulled his lips to hers.

"Zach now, please," she said as she lifted her hips, forcing him further inside of her.

With a final thrust of his hips, Zach was fully inside her. She was warm and slick. Her body wiggled underneath him to force him to move. Not able to take it any longer, Zach began to oblige.

Each thrust caressed Jesse's insides. The feeling was exquisite. The pressure was building and she was sure when she came, she would explode. Wrapping her legs tightly around him she brought her hips up, forcing him to thrust harder.

Jesse could feel it. The end of the tunnel her body was running toward was just around the corner. She grabbed at Zach. Kissed him hard as he pounded into her. It was close; she could feel it.

Jesse closed her eyes and felt Zach give one last deep thrust as she felt her body give in.

When Jesse was breathing normally again, she opened her eyes to see Zach staring down at her.

"Stay away from Hunter," he said.

Jesse smiled sweetly. "Hunter who?"

•

Jesse looked Zach over as they sat outside eating leftovers while the sun set. She loved looking at him.

"Are you mad at me?" Jesse asked.

"Why should I be mad at you?"

He was sitting with his back against the house, his legs stretched out. He was barefoot and wore only his jeans. Jesse sighed as she felt her body respond to his bare chest.

"Well," she said, playing with the food in her plate, "I let you think I had spent the day with Hunter." Jesse didn't really think he was mad, but she wanted him to know she hadn't been with Hunter all day.

"So you weren't with Hunter today?"

"No, I went shopping with Jen."

Zach laughed, realizing everything she'd said today was to get him riled—and it'd worked.

"No," he said, leaning toward her and kissing her lightly. "I'm not mad at you."

Jesse smiled. "So you'll go to the rodeo with me?"

Zach laughed. She didn't give up.

When he started to put his shoes on, Jesse had to think quick. She walked to the stairs and stopped.

"Can't you stay a little while longer?"  She unbuttoned her shirt and let it slide off.  "The view may not be as good as the one from your bed, but I don't think in this case it'll matter." With that, Jesse turned and went up the stairs.

Zach was not a stupid man. Once he could move, he followed her up the stairs, the view being the last thing on his mind.

# Chapter Fifteen

*J*esse had done some online research about the rodeo, and looked up information on Hunter and the other competitors. She had to admit Hunter's resume was pretty impressive. He was a two-time world champion bull rider, and had competed both in the states and abroad. He'd been injured several times, nothing serious, mostly broken bones, but that still sounded like it hurt. He's never been married and was a favorite on the rodeo circuit. She couldn't wait to see him ride.

Since Jesse didn't have much to do and didn't want to sit around, she drove over to Zach's to ride Ty. Not seeing anyone around when she got to there, she took Ty out of his pasture and brought him in the barn to get ready.

She hadn't seen Zach since they'd spent the night together and was a little nervous. Twice now they'd slept together, and although she didn't expect Zach to declare his love, she wasn't sure what he thought or where things might be going.

"So what do you think, Ty?" Jesse asked while running a brush over his back. "You know him better than I do. Should I act like nothing happened and see where it goes? Or should I mention something about what's been going on between us and see what he says? Maybe invite him over again?"

Jesse stopped brushing and looked at him as if she was expecting an answer, but Ty wasn't being much help.

"I think I should just try to act somewhat normal and see where it goes."

*Straight to bed is where it's been going.*

Ty nudged Jesse, which she interpreted as a yes from the horse. Giving him a treat, she finished brushing him just as Zach walked into the barn leading Star. The sight of him made Jesse's heart race. He was wearing worn jeans with a black T-shirt that stretched across his chest and his cowboy hat. Jesse thought he look even sexier than ever, if that was possible.

As bold as she normally was around Zach, Jesse suddenly felt very shy.

Zach put Star in the wash stall next to Ty, then walked over to Jesse and put his hand under her chin to lift her head, and with a smile that touched his eyes, he brought his lips to hers for a kiss.

What Zach had meant to be a light kiss turned into a something deeper once his lips touched hers. Jesse seemed to always initiate contact between the two of them, now it was his turn. Snaking his other arm around her waist, he pulled Jesse toward him until her body was flush against his.

"Hey there," he said, his blue eyes sparkling.

When Zach had come over the hill and seen Jesse's truck in front of the barn his heart had begun to beat faster, and without thought he, nudged Star into a canter trying to get there quicker. When he walked into the barn, a feeling he didn't recognize consumed him when he saw her.

Jesse's knees were weak, and when Zach stepped away, she had to lean on Ty and catch her breath. Zach smelled of horses and sweat and it was all she could do to stop herself from leaping on him.

Zach took the saddle off Star and carried it into the tack room. Watching him walk away, Jesse gave him a slow appraisal. The muscles in his arms were bulging from the weight of the saddle, and the chaps he had on framed his butt, making Jesse want to reach out and grab it.

She thought back to the other night when she did have her hands on him, helping drive him into her.

When Zach stepped back out of the tack room, Jesse leapt on him. Wrapping her legs around him she clasped her hands behind his head and pulled his mouth to hers for a kiss that was passionate, possessive and demanding.

Zach wrapped his arms around Jesse, settling his hands on her ass and holding her to him. He hadn't been expecting her to leap on him, but he was definitely pleased.

She was kissing him in a way that was telling him it didn't matter where they were, she wanted him as much as he wanted her.

"Ah, excuse me."

Jesse froze at the sound of a voice. She opened her eyes to look into Zach's laughing ones. Sure, he *would* think having someone walk in while she was all over him was funny.

"Zach, just wanted to let you know I was finished up out here and was headed home."

Jesse jumped off him.

"Thanks Bob. See ya Monday."

Laughing, Zach looked at Jesse, who was beet red with embarrassment.

"Where are you going? He's gone." Zach reached for Jesse.

"Laugh all you want." She jumped out of his reach. She put her head in her hands and shook her head. "What is wrong with me?"

"Absolutely nothing, darlin," Zach said with a grin.

Jesse felt the rush of heat to her face as she walked away to get Ty's saddle. Trying to regain her composure and what dignity she had left, Jesse gathered what she needed before exiting the tack room.

"I was hoping we could go to the rodeo a little early. I wanted to see Hunter before the events begin."

Zach stopped brushing Star to look at her. "Why would you want to see Hunter?"

"To wish him luck." She stopped to adjust the bridle straps. "I know how good he is, but a little extra support never hurts."

"Hunter gets wished enough luck from all his buckle bunnies."

Jesse walked over to stand near Star's head. "They don't want to wish him luck, they just want to get in his pants."

Zach looked at her, his eyes suddenly hard. "And what about you?"

Jesse was taken aback. "Excuse me?"

"You heard me. You said you would stay away from Hunter."

"I never said any such thing."

Zach gave a snort and, shaking his head, turned his back to Jesse as he continued to brush Star.

"Wait. You think—" Jesse suddenly had a sinking feeling inside. "You've got to be joking! After what just happened, you think I want to have sex with Hunter?"

Zach just shrugged his shoulders.

"Turn around and look at me," she said angrily as she grabbed his arm.

When he turned to face her, Jesse saw something on his face. Contempt maybe?

"So if I decide to go and see Hunter, are you going to stop spending time with me?" Jesse asked, her voice starting to quiver as she tried to keep her emotions under control.

Zach looked down at Jesse. "After the past few days I wouldn't think it wouldn't be such a hard choice." Zach eyes bore into her. "But I know how some women are. They like to try a few cowboys out first."

Jesse stepped back as if she had been hit. Suddenly ill, she was sure she was going to throw up. Confusion and hurt raced through her mind. Where was this coming from? She understood Zach had past relationship issues, but she wasn't about to become the person he was going to take his anger out on.

For her, this fight and relationship or whatever this was between them, were over.

Turning, she unhooked Ty and led him to his stall. Then without looking back, walked out of the barn.

"Damn!" Zach yelled, startling Star. He knew without

going outside—she was gone. He heard the car door slam and the tires on the gravel as she left.

Throwing down the brush he'd been holding, he grabbed Star and led her to a stall.

"Sorry girl," he said, patting her neck.

When Zach had come into the barn and kissed Jesse, he realized he was falling in love with her.

She was smart, fun, beautiful and above all, honest. When she mentioned wanting to see Hunter, Zach's fears took root. Great sex or not, he wasn't getting hurt again.

He leaned his forehead against Star's neck. "What am I gonna do now?"

# Chapter Sixteen

*J*esse cried all the way back to the house. She couldn't believe he had actually made her choose. At any minute she was expecting him to say "just kidding." But he didn't, so she chose. She wouldn't let him dictate who she could be friends with, male or female.

When she first dated Paul, she gave up several male friends because he felt it was inappropriate, yet he continued to have female friends. Jesse cut herself off from people she'd known for years just to make him happy. Granted, she'd only known Hunter a short time, but that wasn't the point.

Once she finished with the tears, she got mad.

What had she done to make him think she was just using him? She'd spent the last two weeks throwing herself at him, and he thought she was just in it for a quickie? Did she look that shallow? And today in the barn. Had that not shown him what she was feeling for him?

Jesse knew the answer. They both had felt the strong attraction to each other, and whereas Jesse had finally decided not to let it scare her and act on it, Zach had acted on it then got scared.

Getting off her bed, she went to get in the shower. There was no way she would sit here alone all night thinking about this. If she did, she would die.

Instead she got ready and went to the rodeo. She hoped she'd be able to find Hunter. He'd told her to find him, but what if he was with someone? She really had no desire to hang around with a bunch of women who were throwing themselves at him.

After asking where she could find the rodeo participants, Jesse made her way around to the gate the riders entered through. There were several women standing around. Some young and pretty, some older ones with obvious miles on them.

Jesse approached the gate person and asked if there was a way she could get a message to Hunter.

The wannabe cowboy guard, a middle-aged man with slicked back hair that was poorly covering his bald spots, just looked her up an down and said, "No one gets back there without an escort or a pass."

"I'm not asking you to let me back there without an escort or pass. I am asking you to see if you can find Hunter for me," Jesse asked, trying to keep herself downwind from the man.

"You and most of the women here are looking for Hunter," he said, then turned to spit tobacco. Jesse stepped back repulsed and looked back at the other women. Were they all really here for Hunter?

"Look," Jesse said, getting as close to the man as she could take. "You either find Hunter for me, or I will make sure the next time the rodeo is in town you'll be the one picking up after the bulls."

The "guard" just looked at her.

"Fine," he said. "But don't expect to make good on that promise when no one comes for you." He picked up his radio and called for someone to find Hunter.

Jesse turned as one of the women spoke to her. "You're wasting your time, honey. Hunter doesn't like any company until after he rides." The woman was probably Jesse's age but looked much older. Her hair was a curly brown and she wore thick makeup to try and hide the lines in her face. Her shirt was so tight Jesse was sure the buttons would pop off. Had Hunter slept with this woman? Surely he had better taste than that.

Jesse just smiled. "Thanks, but he's expecting me." At least Jesse hoped he was. What if he'd forgotten about her? Jesse's worries were cut short when she heard Hunter's voice.

"Jesse," he said, giving her a huge smile. Jesse walked through the gate giving the guard a smug look, and hugged Hunter.

"You made it."

"I wouldn't have missed it for anything."

"I have to finish signing in." He took her hand. "And then I'll show you around."

Jesse felt better already. She was glad she had come rather than sit at home and dwell on what happened with Zach. She couldn't change how he felt, nor would she try. She had worked hard to convince herself it was okay to be who she was. She was done changing who she was to please someone else. She was a good person, an honest person, and if Zach couldn't see that, it was his loss.

•

Zach had actually been excited about going to the rodeo, but then he'd fought with Jesse. He thought about not going, but Alex was riding and his nephew was looking forward to him being there. He hadn't seen Alex ride in a long time and the boy was getting up in the ranks. Zach couldn't let him down. He also wanted to see if Jesse was there. He needed to talk to her and explain.

When he found her, she was sitting up in the stands with Hunter. Zach could tell by the way Hunter was gesturing toward the ring that he was explaining something about the broncs. She was smiling and listening intently, those brown eyes shining up at him. *That should be me*, Zach thought.

Zach thought about today in the barn, but instead of seeing himself kissing Jesse, he saw Hunter in his place. He turned away from them to see his brother walking toward him.

Reese held out his hand. "So Alex wasn't lying, you *are* here." Zach took his brother's hand and shook it. He hadn't seen his brother in several weeks, so although Zach wasn't overjoyed about being here, at least he'd gotten to see Reese.

"Where's your lady friend? Alex said you had a date."

Zach nodded toward Hunter and Jesse.

"What's she doing up there with Hunter?" Reese asked.

"Change of plans. Seems like she prefers the rodeo star." Zach turned and walked away. Reese followed.

"What'd you do this time?" he asked.

"Why is it that I had to have done something?"

"Because I know you. So if she's up there with Hunter instead of you, it means you did something."

Zach gave him an angry look. "Leave it alone."

Reese held up his hands. "If you say so."

•

Jesse had put Zach out of her mind, sort of, and was having a great time with Hunter. He was wonderful at explaining all the rules to her, and had stories about most of the riders.

She grinned as one little boy stopped to ask Hunter for his autograph. The worship in his eyes was evident. It amazed Jesse how Hunter took the time to answer all the boy's questions and take a photo. *I'm with a real celebrity*, Jesse thought.

Jesse grinned at Hunter.

"What?" he asked, seeing the silly grin on her face.

"You're just a big kid. You like talking to the kids more than the adults."

"What can I say?" He shrugged. "It keeps me young." Standing, Hunter held his hand out to her. "Come on, let's get something to eat. Then I have to get ready."

Jesse took his hand as he led her away from the stands to the food booths. Sitting at a table, Jesse picked at her food. She really wasn't hungry. Her stomach was still in knots over the fight she had with Zach. She started to tell Hunter she was done, but stopped when she saw Zach.

Hunter turned to see what, or who, had caught Jesse's attention. "Want to tell me what's going on with you two?" he asked. "I thought you were coming here together."

"We were. We got into an argument," she said. "Over you."

Jesse felt like she owed Hunter an explanation. She didn't want him to think she was just using him, or that her intentions were more than they were.

Hunter just raised his eyebrows. "Do tell," he said, folding his arms across his chest.

Jesse nibbled on her fries, thinking about what to say. She took a deep breath. She didn't want to cry in front of Hunter.

"I told Zach I wanted to see you before you rode, to wish you luck and thank you again for the tickets. He got mad and accused me of 'trying a few cowboys out.' He made me choose—between you or him."

Hunter leaned forward resting his elbows on his knees. "And you chose me?"

Jesse gave him a small smile. "You're surprised?" she asked.

"A little," Hunter admitted. "Jesse, I'm interested in you, but I make no promises to anyone. You should know that about me."

"And that's why it would never work between us," Jesse said. "Don't get me wrong. You are definitely a woman's wet dream come true. But even though I'm not looking for anyone, I just can't be with someone and wonder who they might be with the next night."

Hunter had to laugh. "Honestly Jesse, I'm attracted to you not just because you're beautiful, but I also like you because you don't like me. You talk to me like I'm just a normal guy. I can tell your interest in what I'm saying is genuine. Most of the women you see here are just looking to find themselves a rodeo cowboy. I'm not saying I don't enjoy myself, but it gets old."

Jesse felt relieved. "I just didn't want you to think I was using you to make Zach jealous. I really wanted to come tonight to see you, with or without Zach." Jesse looked over at Zach. "If he can't trust me and let me have the friends I want, then I'd rather be without him." Jesse felt her heart tear when she said that, but it was true.

Hunter stood. "How about we go ride those bulls?"

Jesse took his hand and smiled. She felt better talking to Hunter about just being friends, and was glad he was okay with that. She didn't think she could handle losing two people in one day.

Jesse cheered as Hunter rode and stayed on for eight seconds before half jumping, half getting thrown from the bull. She jumped up to hug him when he came out. "That was unbelievable. Say you'll teach me."

Hunter laughed, her excitement was contagious. "We'll see," he said, draping his arm around her shoulders.

As they walked, Jesse asked him a million questions about what it felt like on the bull. "Does your neck hurt? Your back must kill from twisting like that. Will you be sore tomorrow?" She went on and on, Hunter answering her between laughs.

"Seems like you've found your next cowboy."

Jesse stiffened at the sound of Zach's voice. Turning she saw him standing with Jeremy and Alex, and another man Jesse didn't know.

"Just like all women. They test the waters with one then move onto the next," he said, his glare making her feel small.

Jesse felt Hunter start to move toward Zach. She grabbed his arm, and when he looked down at her, she shook her head. Letting Hunter's arm go, she walked toward Zach with both hurt and love inside her. Jesse's eyes never left Zach's as she stopped in front of him.

"You have to go through the bad ones to get to the better one," Jesse answered before hauling off and slapping him across the face.

As she turned to walk away, Jesse let the tears run down her cheeks. She leaned against her truck cradling her throbbing hand.

Hunter reached out to wipe a tear from her face. "I'm sorry Jesse. I shouldn't have given you those tickets. I—"

She looked up at him and she could see the concern in his eyes.

"No," she said, raising her hand on his cheek. "It's not your fault. You're a better man than you or anyone else gives you credit for."

Hunter opened the truck door. "Make sure you put some ice on that when you get home."

Zach turned to see his brother and nephews gaping at him open-mouthed. He couldn't believe he'd said those things to Jesse, but when he saw her hugging Hunter and laughing, the words just came out.

"I'm going home," he said and turned to feel a fist connect with his jaw, sending him falling onto his butt.

"What's your problem, Baker?" Hunter yelled. Once Jesse drove off, he'd let the anger come. "I may enjoy a lot of women, but at least I know how to treat them. God only knows why she loves you."

Zach watched Hunter walk away and turned to see his brother and nephews do the same. Obviously, they felt as Hunter did, and he couldn't blame them.

# Chapter Seventeen

Zach couldn't remember when he'd been more miserable. His jaw had stopped aching days ago, but the rest of him still hurt. He knew he had to straighten things out with Jesse, not just because he'd been an ass, but because he missed her.

His grandfather had come out the day after the rodeo and given him a tongue lashing that made Zach feel like he was ten again. He'd been embarrassed by the way he'd acted, and should have known once his grandfather found out he'd be in for it.

"I can't believe a grandson of mine would treat a woman like that. I don't care what you think she did. You just made yourself look like a fool."

Zach had to agree. He was sure most of, if not all of the town, knew about what he had said. So he stayed away from town and specifically the diner. He couldn't face Jesse, not until he figured out what to say to her.

Hunter's words kept running through his head. Hunter said Jesse loved him. He still wasn't sure what he felt for Jesse, actually he was sure, he just couldn't come to terms with it.

After a week of not leaving the ranch, Zach got his courage up to go into town. When he walked in the diner he was relieved as well as disappointed that Jesse wasn't here.

Jen came to take his order, angry eyes flashing at him.

"Look, I know I'm an ass," he said. "Can I just have some coffee?"

Jen brought the coffee over and although Zach hated to ask

he did. "Do you know where I can find Jesse? I'd thought she'd be here."

"And what is it you'd want Jesse for?"

"I just need to talk to her. I went by her place the past few mornings and she wasn't there."

Jen looked Zach over. He knew he looked pretty bad. She could probably see the circles under his eyes and the troubled look on his face.

"She's over in Jackson at Rivergate farm. She's been giving some lessons and has a horse there she's trying out."

Zach was relieved she was still around. He had actually worried that she'd either left or gone on the circuit with Hunter.

"Thanks." He got up to leave. He had to get this over with.

•

Jesse couldn't have felt better. She flew over the jump and smiled. The gelding was smooth.

After some research, she'd found there was a small hunter barn about forty-five minutes from Dillon. She'd driven out and talked to the owner, Gail. They'd hit it off and Gail asked if Jesse wanted to give some lessons. There wasn't a huge market for English riding lessons in the area, but those who did want to give it a try came to Gail's.

The stable had about seven horses, but none were what Jesse wanted for herself. She looked online and was able to find a gorgeous dark chestnut gelding with white socks that would be perfect. She'd had the horse, whose name was Gator, brought over to Gail's for a trial, and he was turning out to be wonderful.

Jesse stopped to catch her breath and directed her attention to the other rider in the ring.

"Get your lead," she yelled. "Don't let him rush like that, you won't get your striding."

Jesse had five students. Three were under the age of ten, and the other two were teenagers. She loved spending time with the kids. The fact she could help them achieve their riding goals made Jesse feel useful. She went home knowing she made a difference.

Sometimes, like today, she would ride with her older students. It made the lesson more fun and she found she benefited as well as her students.

Carrie was one of the better riders and Jesse enjoyed working with her. If she ended up buying the gelding she would probably ask Carrie to ride him in some local horse shows for her. When the girl was done with her round, she stopped next to Jesse.

"Looks like we have an audience today," Carrie said nodding her head toward the barn.

Jesse looked over and her heart stopped when she saw Zach. It had been over a week since the rodeo, and she had worked hard to put him out of her mind and a wall around her heart.

She'd gone to the diner for breakfast every morning before coming out here and had finally stopped waiting for him to walk in. Now here he was.

"Let's finish up," Jesse said, turning away from Zach.

Carrie gave her a jumping course and Jesse took off. She needed to stay focused on what she was doing, then she could worry about Zach.

Zach watched as Jesse got direction from the other girl. He saw her look at him then turn away. He hoped it was because she was riding and not because she didn't want to see him. He held his breath as she took off toward the jumps. He didn't know much about jumping but could tell Jesse was a capable rider.

The gelding flew over the first two jumps effortlessly. When he stumbled in front of the next one Zach's heart jumped to his throat. Jesse collected the horse enough to make it over the jump, and Zach saw her shake her head and circle back. When she approached the jump this time, the horse was perfect.

When she finished, she went back over to the other rider and he could see her pointing to the jumps. The other girl smiled and nodded then walked her horse toward the barn. After dismounting and giving Zach the once-over, she led her horse in.

Jesse took a breath. Best get this over with. She knew she would see Zach sooner or later, but he'd caught her off guard by coming here.

Still on Gator, she rode over and stood in front of Zach, her heart beating so hard she was sure he could hear it.

Zach looked up to meet her gaze. "You look great out there. Ty's going to be sad he's been replaced. He's beautiful." Zach patted the gelding.

Jesse jumped down and looked at him. "Why are you here Zach?"

"Jesse." Zach ran his hand through his hair. He thought he had what he would say all planned out. "Can we talk?"

With him standing in front of her, she was unable to keep that wall up and the hurt leaked out.

Jesse looked at him. Part of her was curious and wanted to hear what he had to say, the other part told her to tell him to leave.

"Let me put him away," she said, motioning to Gator.

It wasn't the warmest reception, but Zach would take it. At least she was willing to talk to him.

Rather than just watch, Zach picked up a brush and started brushing the horse after Jesse removed the saddle.

"Where'd you get him?"

"Over in Billings. I found him online, and had him brought over," she answered, not looking at him. Jesse picked up a brush and started on the other side. "I wanted to keep busy. The builder said it would be a few weeks before he had everything together, and even then it would be awhile before my own place would be ready."

When they finished, Jesse took Gator and let him loose in the pasture. He stopped to nuzzle her and she gave him a treat before walking off.

"Well, here we go," she said to herself before turning and

walking over to Zach.

They stood watching Gator graze, and Jesse waited for Zach to speak. She wasn't about to start the conversation or make it easy for him. She watched him out of the corner of her eye and could tell he was thinking carefully about what to say.

Even as angry and hurt as she was, Jesse was still attracted to him. For a split second she thought about letting him off the hook and telling him they would just put that night behind them, but she couldn't do that. If he wanted her back, even as a friend, he needed to apologize and even then Jesse wasn't sure how she'd feel.

"Jesse, I—" Zach began. He turned to face her. "I guess I should start by saying I'm sorry."

He looked at her and she could see that he was. His normally sparkling blue eyes looked tired and sad. Instead of standing tall, his posture was slightly slumped. He looked like she felt. She could feel tears forming in her eyes.

"I was a jerk. It was wrong of me to say those things to you. I know there is no excuse, but I hope that with time you'll be able to forgive me."

Jesse looked at him. "What is it about Hunter you don't like?"

"It's not that I don't like him. When I saw you at the diner, I got jealous. Then when you talked about seeing him I got scared. My actions were a way of protecting myself."

Jesse waited.

"Jesse, there is part of my past I don't talk about. A relationship I thought was it for me. I got hurt because I trusted someone. I believed things she told me. I swore I would never let anyone get that close again."

"I don't understand what this has to do with Hunter."

"When I left the city and came back here, Lisa would call me, trying to get me to come back. When I wouldn't, she switched tactics. She'd met Hunter in the past and started to contact him. She tried to make me think something was going on between them to make me jealous. Hunter told me nothing ever happened. He couldn't be bothered with someone he called a vindictive bitch. I believed him. We'd grown up like brothers. I knew I could trust him."

"Then why do you think he would do that to you now? That I would do that to you?" she asked.

"I knew he wouldn't." He met her eyes. "And deep down I knew you wouldn't either. I wasn't sure what was going on with us, how you felt about us, how I felt about you," he said softly.

"So you thought I would try to make you jealous? To trap you?"

Jesse shook her head and took a step away from him. "After what I told you about my ex and what was going on between us?"

She wasn't exactly yelling at him, but her tone told Zach she was angry.

"I may not be the best at relationships, but I could swear what we had was more than just physical."

Zach felt like an idiot. He knew he had no reason to be suspicious of her and Hunter, but his past always got in the way. Moving to stand in front of her, Zach lifted her face to look at him.

"I was wrong," he said, wanting to hang his head but looked her in the eye instead.

Jesse turned away from him and looked across the field. She knew she loved Zach. Even before they'd fought, she knew it. Zach understood her, supported her, listened to her. The strong physical attraction was just a bonus.

Jesse never thought she would ever hurt as much as she did right now. She wanted to forgive Zach, but now she was the scared one.

"Jesse, please tell me you might be able to forgive me?"

She turned back to him. "Putting me in the same category as your old girlfriend or those rodeo groupies was low. I trusted you. I loved you."

Jesse struggled to keep her voice steady, but tears welled in her eyes. She turned to face him.

"You made me feel like dirt. You made the nights we spent together seem like you'd spent them with the local slut."

Zach wanted to look away. He didn't want to see the hurt in her eyes, hurt he'd put there.

Jesse walked away. That was all she could take for one day. Hearing the reason why Zach acted the way he did didn't make it any easier.

"Jesse," he said, grabbing her arm.

Jesse jerked her arm back and turned to him. At that moment, with him looking at her with pleading eyes, she realized there would be no way she could stay mad at him. Her heart wouldn't let her.

"I can't say I forgive you Zach, not yet. You really hurt me," Jesse paused as tears ran down her cheeks. "I refuse to put myself in a situation where it might happen again. Hunter's my friend and not you or anyone else will tell me to stay away from him."

Jesse turned and headed back toward the barn.

Well, at least she'd spoken to him. It was a start. He knew it would take awhile to gain her trust back, but he was willing to work at it.

She'd said she loved him. He wasn't sure if she realized what she'd said, but he didn't care. She had said it. That alone made him determined to win her back.

Jesse felt better than she had in days. On the way home Hunter called and she told him about Zach.

"So things are better between you two?" he asked.

"Yes, but it still hurts. At least he knows that if he wants to be part of my life he'll have to accept that you are, too."

# Chapter Eighteen

When Jesse stepped outside to have her morning coffee, she stopped and stared. On the deck table was a beautiful bunch of wildflowers tied with a ribbon.

*Zach*. She picked them up and smiled. He was really trying to make an effort.

The dogs came bounding up the stairs looking for breakfast. "Some watch dogs you are, you didn't even hear him out here."

The next three mornings were the same. When Jesse came outside there were flowers on the table. She could get used to this.

The following morning Jesse got up expected to see her flowers on the table, but was pleasantly surprised to see that along with the flowers was Zach.

"I didn't think you'd ever get up," he said smiling.

"Fridays are my off day, so I sleep in."

Zach already knew this; he'd asked Jen what days Jesse didn't go and ride.

She sat down across from him. "Thank you for my flowers. You do know I'll be expecting them every morning now."

"Until the first snow, I'll see what I can do." Zach motioned to the dogs. "When did they get here?"

"About two weeks ago. They've already been reprimanded for their lack of watchdog skills. They never heard you out here."

The dogs came running up the stairs and stopped, because

they'd finally realized there was a stranger there. Roxy barked wildly at him, but kept her distance. Boomer decided to do what he always did and hide behind Jesse.

"Don't bother," Jesse said when Zach tried to pet Roxy. "She'll come to you when she's ready."

"What are your plans for today?" he asked.

"Laundry, cleaning, the usual day-off stuff."

"Feel like taking a ride with me to go look at some horses?"

Jesse looked at him over the rim of her mug. He looked like he had gotten some sleep, and the sparkle was back in his eyes. Jesse had to admit he looked good.

"Sure, where we going?" Jesse asked.

"Wyoming."

"Wyoming?"

"Yeah, it's only a few hours drive and I work with another rancher there. He's got a few horses in he thought might work for your program."

"Give me a half hour to get ready," Jesse said, standing to go inside.

Zach smiled at her and picked up a tennis ball he'd seen on the ground. "Take your time. I'm going to work on winning over your dogs."

•

Zach glanced over at Jesse while he drove. He'd been a little nervous about asking her to go with him this morning. He really thought she might say no. He wanted to show her she could trust him again.

He asked about the two additional kittens he saw roaming around her house.

Jesse smiled. "I seem to have developed a habit of stopping by the shelter at least once a week. Sampson and Delilah were the last in the litter. I couldn't leave them there."

"Sampson and Delilah? And you already have Romeo and Juliet. Who's next?"

"Another great couple in love." She paused and grinned at

him. "Mickey and Minnie."

Zach laughed and asked about Gator and her lessons.

"He's really great. I've decided to buy, and will keep him at Gail's until my own barn is ready."

"Has the builder given you an estimate when yours might be ready?" he asked.

"They're trying to get everything together to break ground in the next few weeks to get the pipe work in. He said once the snow came it would be more difficult."

Jesse was having a hard time believing it could be snowing in a few month there. She used to think the summers in Connecticut were too hot and long. Now she had a feeling she'd be wishing for those long summers.

Zach asked her more questions about the building plans.

"I've talked to Gail about bringing her students over. It would allow her to teach through the winter and have access to more horses."

Jesse went on to tell him about some of the therapy programs she'd contacted in the area.

Zach smiled. The fact she was sharing her plans with him told him she was becoming comfortable with him again.

When they crossed over into Wyoming, Jesse commented on the land. "I thought Montana was beautiful. I can't believe this is out here untouched. It's wonderful."

Zach agreed. Montana and the surrounding states were some of the most beautiful in the U.S.

They were greeted by Zach's friend, Randy, when they reached his ranch. Zach walked with him to look at several young horses in the corral while Jesse wondered around.

"Randy wants to know if I'd like to try out a couple of the horses. Do you want to ride?" Zach asked Jesse.

"Sure."

Once mounted, they headed off across a field toward some mountains. Zach explained to her that this was the same mountain line that ran up to Montana and around their land. Jesse let herself relax. She'd been a little nervous about spending the day with Zach. Ever since he had come out to Gail's she hadn't been able to stop thinking about him.

He'd hurt her and said he was sorry. She believed he was. Zach was not the type of person to use words to get what he wanted. If he didn't feel it, he didn't say it.

She loved him. She couldn't stop herself. Zach was everything in a man she'd ever wanted. Jesse didn't think she would ever want to be in a serious relationship again, but now she couldn't see herself without Zach.

When they rode up to a lake at the base of the mountains, she was stunned to see a blanket and picnic spread out.

"Hungry?" he asked.

Jesse's heart swelled. Never before had anyone done anything like this for her.

"Not sure what we'll find in here. I don't think Randy is much of a cook." Zach opened the basket.

"Whatever is in there will be fine," was all Jesse could say.

The basket ended up having sandwiches, some fruit and some of the best chocolate chip cookies she'd ever had. This was the stuff Jesse's dreams were made of.

•

Zach lay back on the blanket with his hands behind his head and watched Jesse walk around the lake shore. He noticed how she didn't care if her jeans got dirty or wet. She didn't hesitate to pick up a rock or stick, throwing them into the lake. He smiled at how she seemed to take pleasure in just being here.

Jesse walked to the blanket and lay on her stomach next to Zach. Laying her head on her arms she looked up to meet his eyes. "When I kiss you Zach, when you touch me, when I look at you, something inside me comes alive."

"Jesse, I—"

"No," she said touching her finger to his lips knowing he was about to apologize. "It's okay. I've never been one to stay angry, even when I get hurt. I've put it behind me—to dwell on it would just make it keep hurting. Will you do one thing for me though?"

"Anything."

"Tell me about Lisa," she asked.

Zach's jaw tightened and he looked away. He had been trying to put all thoughts of Lisa behind him. She was the reason Zach had such a hard time accepting Jesse for who she was.

Everytime Jesse did something that pulled at his heart, he immediately thought of Lisa and how she had once led him to believe she wanted to be part of his life in Dillon.

He turned his head to look at Jesse and what he saw in her eyes was an honesty that had always been there—he had just never let himself see it.

"I met Lisa through Reese's wife, Lori." Zach closed his eyes remembering. He could see Lisa. Her long brown hair swept back over her shoulders. Her makeup perfectly applied. Her outfit tailor-made.

"She and Lori had gone to college together. They shared an apartment until Lori and Reese were married. We met at the wedding. I still had a few months left of school. She already had a job over in Butte. We kept in touch by phone, got together when we could. When I graduated, she persuaded me to move to Butte instead of returning to Dillon."

"Persuade you? How does one persuade Zach Baker to do something?" Jesse asked, smiling.

Zach grinned and reached over to run a finger over Jesse's lips. "Remind me to show you later. She was already on her way up the corporate ladder of a stock trading company," he said, returning to the story. "She assured me once she'd established more clients, she'd be able to move to Dillon."

Zach gave a small laugh. "One year turned into two. She kept promising it wouldn't be much longer. I hated living in the city. I grew up on a hundred acres and longed to have land of my own. The confines of the city were getting to me."

Jesse watched the play of emotions go across Zach's face. He would smile as if remembering the good times, but then frown because there seemed to be more bad than good.

She wanted to hear from him what caused him to become so distrustful of relationships. She didn't blame him. On the contrary, she understood. Her own past relationship had taught her that as much as you want something to work, sometimes it just doesn't.

"I should have realized she never planned to move. She was all city. She loved the night life, the busy schedule. When we visited my parents she would always keep her distance from anything that would ruin her manicure," he said, taking Jesse's hand and looking at it. "There is no way you can live on a ranch and not break some nails." Still holding her hand he went on. "We were already having problems when Lori left Reese. She, too, had been a city girl, but she had tried to make it work with him. They were together six years. I'm sure Lori confided in Lisa about how unhappy she was. Lori only confirmed what Lisa had already knew—she would never be happy living anywhere but in the city."

Zach's voice sounded sad, as if he thought it was his fault he couldn't make Lisa happy.

"It was hard for me to trust you, Jesse. When I'd listen to you talk about living on your ranch, about doing the things I also loved to do, I got scared. Lisa told me the same things. But with you I should have realized you weren't lying, that you truly want the same things I do. I'm sorry."

Jesse looked at Zach and could see he was sorry. She saw the disappointment he felt from Lisa and the sadness he felt.

"You loved her," Jesse said. "It's amazing how much of yourself you'll give up, and the things you'll overlook in order to not lose someone."

Zach looked over at Jesse. He loved her. His feelings for Jesse were stronger than they'd ever been for Lisa. Jesse was the other half of him. She was what he'd been waiting for to help him heal.

Jesse leaned over and touched her lips to Zach's. She hadn't realized how much she'd missed him. Zach opened his mouth, allowing Jesse to take charge of the kiss. Pulling her on top of him, he ran his fingers into her hair, holding her face as they kissed.

"I'm in love with you, Jesse," he said when their lips parted.

Jesse's heart skipped a beat.

"When?" she asked. "When did you know you loved me?"

Zach thought back and smiled. "It probably started the day after I met you, when you came to the ranch to ride. You were standing with Ty. Your face was against his," he said, pushing a strand of hair behind her ear. "You were smiling. The look on your face was one of pure joy." Zach could see it in his mind as if it were yesterday. "Then the night you helped me deliver the foal. I had the same feeling when I looked at you. And when we made love—" He ran a thumb over her lower lip. "The connection I felt with you was something I'd never felt."

Zach frowned. "When we fought, it tore at my insides that I'd just ruined what we had. The thought that you hated me, that I would never get to hold you again, it ate at me. I couldn't stand it. I didn't want to be without you."

Bringing his lips to hers, Zach gave Jesse such a soft, gentle kiss that Jesse was sure she could feel the love flowing from it.

"And when was it that you knew you loved me?" he asked, smiling.

"What makes you think I love you?"

"You told me, the day I came to apologize."

Jesse grinned. "Caught that, did you?"

"It's the one thing I heard loud and clear."

Jesse kissed Zach slowly, savoring his lips on hers. Feeling every inch of his body against hers. She'd put everything that happened between them behind her and was living for the moment.

They both ignored the rumble of thunder in the distance. When rain drops started to hit Jesse's back, she reluctantly looked up. Dark storm clouds were rolling toward them.

"Time to go?"

"Time to go." Zach kissing her thoroughly one more time

before getting up.

Jesse mounted her horse and watched as Zach tied the picnic items to his saddle. She couldn't help but wonder how she got so lucky. The fight between them had actually brought them closer.

When Zach was on his horse, he held his hand out to her. Placing her hand in his, Zach brought it to his lips and smiled.

Jesse's heart swelled. What she felt for Zach was both overwhelming and consuming, and she wouldn't give it up for anything in the world.

# Chapter Nineteen

*J*esse looked down at herself. Jen told her the outfit she'd chosen would be fine, but Jesse wasn't used to wearing such revealing clothes.

"You planning on picking someone up tonight?" Hunter asked from the doorway of her room.

Blushing Jesse looked at herself in the mirror. "Too much?" she asked, still concerned she would stick out.

"Not at all." He came to stand behind her. "You look beautiful."

Jesse smiled back at him. Hunter had come into town that morning. He had a four-day break from the rodeo and wanted to take some time and relax.

Things could not have been better between her and Zach. After the day they'd spent in Wyoming, he seemed to understand she didn't want to be hurt, and wouldn't purposely do anything to hurt him. She told Zach that Hunter would be visiting her, and had been relieved to know he was okay with that.

Jesse was so excited about going out. Jen had invited her to go dancing at a local club and she had jumped at the chance to do something fun. The bar was only a few miles out of town, and Jesse was surprised to see how crowded it was.

The club was dark but the lights from the stage helped provide some light. She could see a bar about ten feet or so to the left of the door. The band was set up on the stage at the back of the room, and there was a large dance floor that people were already making use of. Small tables were set up between the bar and the dance floor. Jesse noticed several women looking at Hunter and scowling at her. Ah, to be the envy of every woman. Reaching the table, Jesse sat down next to Jen.

"You look great," Jen said.

"Thanks. I was a little worried, but now seeing how everyone else is dressed, I feel more comfortable."

Hunter brought Jesse a drink and she started to relax some. Zach knew she'd be here tonight, and she was really hoping he'd show up.

"I have to warn you," Jesse said to Jen, "I've never been in a honky tonk bar before, so I might embarrass you."

"No problem," Jen said, taking a drink of her beer. Leaning closer to Jesse she went on, "Jeremy insists on trying to dance and he's horrible. You can't be much worse than he is."

Jesse looked around at the people. She'd never seen so many cowboy hats in one place. There were definitely more women than men, and the women were on the prowl. Most were dressed provocatively with low-cut shirts and very tight jeans.

Turning back to Jen to ask if she'd seen Zach, Jesse was surprised to see Alex had joined them. Alex was identical to Jeremy. His hair was a little longer and a bit disheveled. He had the same beautiful blue eyes that Jeremy and Zach had. The one difference was an arrogance he carried. He reminded Jesse of Hunter, only younger.

"Jesse, this is Alex," Jen said.

"Nice to finally meet you," Jesse said.

"Pleasure," he said with a casual grin.

Jesse was sure that smile brought many a women to their knees. *If I were fifteen years younger I would be one of them*, she thought.

Jesse watched Alex talking to Hunter. Both were oblivious to the sultry stares of the women around them. Jesse turned to comment on this to Jen, and was hauled out of her chair and onto the dance floor.

Jesse was not familiar at all with the song that was playing and had no clue as to the steps of the dance that went along with it. Jesse laughed as she tried hard to pick up the steps and not crush anyone's toes. Relief showed on her face when Alex appeared at her side and tried to show her what to do.

•

When Zach finally saw Jesse he had to do a double-take. He almost didn't recognize her. His sweet Jesse looked anything but sweet tonight. She was smiling up at Alex as she tried to pick up the dance steps. He let his eyes roam over her. Her outfit was enough to turn him hard.

Starting at her cowboy boots, Zach's gaze traveled up to her toned legs and paused briefly to take in the perfect shape of her bottom in the Daisy Duke shorts she had on. Continuing up, his mouth about watered as he looked at her breasts in the snug red top.

Zach watched as a young cowboy started toward her, but stopped when Alex made it there first. The looks Jesse got from other men irritated Zach, but he also knew he had nothing to worry about.

Zach smiled as he remembered their afternoon together. Talking with Jesse about his past relationship seemed to set his heart free.

He saw her smile and stick her tongue out at something Hunter said. Instead of feeling angry or jealous, he felt lucky. He trusted Jesse, and that made him feel better than he'd felt in a long time.

When the song ended, Jesse was laughing so hard her sides hurt. "Thanks for helping me," she said to Alex when they made it back to the table. "I hope I didn't break all your toes."

Alex grinned. "I enjoyed it. Besides, it was fun trying to make my uncle jealous."

"Jealous?"

Alex nodded in the direction of the bar as he picked up his beer. "He's been watching you since he came in."

Jesse looked toward the bar and sure enough, Zach was

looking back at her. The intensity of his gaze gave Jesse a tingling sensation through her body.

Getting a mischievous smile on her face, Jesse got up. "I'll be right back."

Jesse walked to where Zach was standing and leaned on the bar as she waited to order.

Zach smiled. The way she was standing gave him a wonderful view of her backside. When Zach brought his eyes back up, he was looking at the man who had tried to approach Jesse on the dance floor. The man was smiling as he looked Jesse over. When he meet Zach's eyes, his smile faded at the look he was receiving back. Then, giving Zach a nervous nod, he turned and walked away.

"Buy you a drink?" he asked.

Jesse turned her head toward Zach. She slowly looked him over from head to toe before meeting his eyes. The smile she wore indicated she liked was she saw.

"Sure."

Zach ordered two shots of whiskey.

"If a girl didn't know better, I'd say you were hoping to get me drunk." She picked up the glass. Fire shot down her throat and into her gut as she drank the whiskey down.

"Maybe." Zach grinned and downed his own shot. "You here alone?"

Jesse smiled and leaned closer to him, barely touching her lips to his. "Maybe," she answered and walked away.

She stopped about half way through the club and looked back over her shoulder. Running her eyes over him, she smiled and kept walking.

As Zach went to move away from the bar, Alex came up to stand next to him.

"She's really something," Alex said. "Nice body." Alex took a drink and glanced at Zach. "I wonder if she likes younger guys."

Zach just smiled at him. His nephew was trying to get him riled and it wasn't working.

"I can tell you from experience," he said, taking one last swig of his beer before setting it down, "she doesn't."

Zach moved from the bar and followed in the direction Jesse had gone.

She waited at the end of the hall by the bathrooms. She liked playing with Zach and hoped she'd given him enough to make him follow her.

A moment later she looked up to see Zach walking toward her. Her breath caught. His jeans were worn and so soft looking that Jesse ached to run her hands over them. His collared shirt was fit so that Jesse could see the definition of his broad shoulders and tapered waist.

He stopped directly in front of her, placing his hands on either side of her head. Jesse looked up to meet his blue eyes, then let her eyes drop to his lips and instinctively licked hers.

Zach smiled and brought his lips to hers. He was not in the mood to be soft and romantic, and his kiss was meant to be forceful and claiming.

If Jesse hadn't been leaning against the wall she would have slid to the floor. The kiss was making her knees weak, and her body was on fire.

Although she wanted to grab Zach and run her hands over him, she kept her them at her sides, allowing only their lips to touch. When Zach's lips left hers, it took Jesse a minute to regain her composure before she could look up at him. When she did, the look on his face told her the kiss had the same effect on him as it did on her.

Jesse smiled seductively. Kissing him lightly on the lips, she took his bottom lip between her teeth before moving to walk by him and back out to the bar.

Zach looked over his shoulder and watched her go. He couldn't move if he wanted to. If he walked back out into the bar he would be thoroughly embarrassed by the bulge in his jeans.

Jesse made it back to the table and sat. Her legs were like Jell-o and she was hot—and it wasn't from the temperature in the bar. She wanted to rip Zach's clothes off right there, but was having more fun playing with him.

Jen just looked at her with eyebrows raised and a knowing smile.

Jesse saw Zach come out of the hall they'd been in. She watched him walk back to the bar and wondered if she should just leave with him now.

When he reached the bar, Zach turned and gave Jesse a smoldering look that said he was not going to wait much longer.

The band took a break and the DJ took over. Jen grabbed Jesse's hand. "Jeremy won't dance to this stuff," she said, dragging Jesse back out onto the dance floor.

Jesse knew the song. It was a fast moving sexy song by a new girl group. The beat was one that allowed her to move in a provocative manner, which Jesse did rather well after her shot of whiskey and two beers.

Zach was becoming wildly excited by watching Jesse dance. He knew she was dancing for him. She was looking directly at him, and it was taking a lot of control for him not to drag her off the dance floor and out of the bar.

Zach went to stand at the edge of the dance floor near where Jesse danced. When the song ended she came and stood in front of him.

"Take me home, Zach." Her breathing was heavy, from dancing or from what she knew was to come, he wasn't sure.

Zach looked past Jesse to Hunter, who just smiled and raised his drink to him. Without giving her an answer, Zach took her hand and walked out.

When Zach reached his truck, he pinned Jesse against the door, pressing his body against hers. She moaned into his mouth as he kissed her.

Jesse slid her arms around Zach's neck pulling her body up to his. Jesse was so turned on she briefly wondered how hard the truck bed would be.

Removing his lips from Jesse's, Zach opened the truck

door and all but threw her in. When he got behind the wheel he looked at her. She was a fantasy come true. Her lips were swollen, he eyelids low and she looked as if she was about to leap on him. What more could a man want?

•

For Jesse, the drive was taking much too long. The combination of dancing, drinking and kissing had set her libido on fire.

She looked over at Zach and licked her lips. She could already feel his hands running over her, his lips on her body. She was getting herself more and more worked up just by thinking about him.

"How busy is this road?" she asked.

Zach looked at the clock. "There's not much traffic this time of night."

When Zach looked at her she gave him a slow smile then leaned down to take off her boots. He watched as she slipped off one, then the other. She bent over and ran her hands over her legs then sat back and looked at him. With a little smirk and one raised eyebrow, she held his gaze as she started to take off her shirt.

With her boots and shirt off, Jesse crawled closer to Zach. Balancing on her hands and knees she leaned toward over and ran her tongue along his jaw line. Jesse smiled as she felt his jaw tighten.

Talking his earlobe between her teeth she gently tugged and placed her hand between Zach's legs. As she ran light kisses along Zach's neck she felt him getting harder under her caress.

Removing her hand and lips, Jesse sat back and unbuttoned her shorts. Extending her legs, she slid them off as Zach tried to keep the truck straight.

"Jesse," he groaned.

Putting a finger to his lips, Jesse went back to kissing his neck. But instead of replacing her hand where it had been between his legs, she took his right hand off the steering wheel and directed it between her legs. She pressed his palm against her and ground into his hand.

This was more than Zach could take. Pulling the truck over to the side, he was kissing her before it even stopped.

Moaning, Jesse reached for the button on his pants. Lifting his hips, she slid his jeans down. She pulled her lips away and looked at him as she moved to straddle him.

Jesse's breath caught as he entered her. She was so wet he slid in without hesitation. He filled her fully and completely. Just having him inside her made Jesse's body want to explode. With not much room, Jesse slowly moved on him. Up and down. Grinding and pulling.

Zach ran his hands over Jesse's back to her backside. He gripped her as she moved. Zach was no longer concerned about a car coming along. There was absolutely no way he could stop even if he wanted to. Jesse felt incredible on him. Her boldness excited him. Sex with her was like nothing he had ever experienced. She surprised him in more ways than one. He was already attracted to the confident, self-assured, Jesse. But the passionate Jesse blew his mind.

Jesse couldn't feel her body. All she felt was one body — Zach's blended against hers. She clung to him as the sensations built. She wanted to move faster, but instead kept her movements slow, savoring each feeling that came with having Zach inside her. She couldn't seem to get him deep enough in her and pushed against him until she was consumed by him.

When they climaxed together, Jesse cried out. She was breathing heavy, sweaty, and very, very satisfied.

Jesse never gave a second thought to what she was doing. She wanted Zach right there and then. She was tired of waiting for what she wanted. She wanted to experience things she never had.

Having passionate sex in a truck on the side of the road was definitely something she had never experienced, but after tonight, would be something she'd definitely do again.

Jesse leaned her forehead against Zach's and smiled into his eyes.

"Sorry," she said, shrugging her shoulders. "I couldn't wait."

"Not a problem," he said, kissing her. "Not a problem at all."

# Chapter Twenty

*J*esse woke up to the sound of rain hitting the windows in Zach's bedroom. *Zach's bedroom.* She was in Zach's house, in his bed. Jesse smiled to herself. She'd never had a more exciting, erotic night.

Earlier Zach had woken her up to watch the sunrise through the windows. What little they could see through the clouds was beautiful. *I can get used to this.*

They'd made love, and when Zach got up to take care of the horses, he told her to stay in bed and sleep. Snuggled under the covers with the smell of Zach around her, Jesse did just that.

"Hey, sleepy head," Zach said coming out of the bathroom.

Jesse stared. Zach looked to have just gotten out of the shower. His hair was still wet and his jeans were on, but unbuttoned at the top. He had no shirt on and looked incredible. *Will the effect he has on me ever go away?* she wondered.

Zach came over to the bed and gave her a kiss.

"How's your head? Any hangover?"

Jesse stretched and smiled. "Nope. All that exercise must have helped."

Zach gave her a grin. "Good. Hungry?"

Jesse looked him over. "A little."

She leaned up to kiss him, the sheet falling to her waist, exposing her breast, which she pressed against Zach's chest.

His skin was warm from the shower and felt wonderful

against her. Jesse could feel a tingling between her legs.

Zach laughed into her mouth. "You're going to wear me out."

"Not possible." She planted kisses on his face and neck. "Besides, what else do you have to do today?" Jesse let her hand slide over Zach groin. "The horses are fed." Her tongue ran over Zach's lips. "And it's miserable out today. But—" She lay back to stretch, giving Zach full view of her body. "If you'd rather go out and play cowboy, I'll just go."

Jesse started to get up when Zach landed on her.

•

Zach looked down at Jesse. Last night had been amazing. This morning when he got up to feed the horses he was almost afraid to go, thinking she'd be gone when he got back.

When he'd come back, she was lying where he'd left her. She was sleeping on her stomach, the sheet around her waist.

He'd lived in this house for four years and never once had a woman spent the night. Jesse had spent the night twice now, and he wanted her to spend more.

Zach grinned. "Were you planning on walking home in the rain?"

"I could get a ride," she said, lifting her hand to play with the hair at the nape of his neck.

"Really. From who?"

"I'd call Hunter."

"Hunter, huh? I doubt you'll be able to find Hunter until sometime this evening."

Jesse rolled her eyes like she was thinking. "I could call Jen. She'd come and get me."

"You're going to ask Jen to drive all the way out here to drive you down the road to your house?"

Jesse got a mischievous smile on her face. "I'd take Ty."

"You'd steal my horse?" Zach asked laughing.

"Not steal. Borrow. Besides, he'd probably prefer to come and live with me."

"So in order to keep you from stealing my horse, I need to

stay here today? And what would I do all day?"

"Well, if I recall correctly you have quite a few movies we could watch."

"Movies, okay," Zach said, starting to kiss her neck.

"Yes, movies, and I'm sure you must have something to eat here."

"Movies, food. I can do that," he said, moving down to her breasts.

"And, I think I saw some chocolate syrup in the refrigerator the other night."

Zach stopped kissing and looked at her.

Jesse looked back at him and tried not to laugh.

Zach jumped up and started toward the door. "Where are you going?"

"To make sure there is chocolate syrup, and if not, go and get some." With a wink, Zach left the room.

Jesse sank into the bed and waited. Guess she wouldn't be stealing a horse today.

# Chapter Twenty-One

*J*esse sat on the plane flipping through a magazine. She looked over at Emma and saw her daughter was happily watching Barbie save the world. Jesse felt a little guilty about not spending more time at her parents, but she was anxious to get back to Montana. The builders were breaking ground next week and she wanted to spend as much time focusing on Emma as she could.

Emma had been upset when Jesse arrived. Paul had promised to come see her before she left for Montana, but he broke his promise because he and a friend had tickets to a football game.

"It's the first game of the season," Paul had explained. "Tell Emma I'll come out to Montana to see her in a few weeks."

Jesse wanted to tell him not to bother. She wouldn't tell Emma he would come to Montana, because she knew he wouldn't. Emma was finally getting to where she didn't ask for her father as much. It's not that Jesse didn't want her to see him, he just always let her down. So if Emma wanted to talk about him, Jesse listened. If she wanted to call him, Jesse let her. If not, Jesse just left it alone.

The plane started to descend. Jesse took Emma's hand in hers and smiled.

Emma took her headphones off and looked out the window. "Are we there?"

"Yes, we're here."

Emma turned to look out the window. "Mommy, look at the

mountains. It looks like we're flying right next to them."

Jesse leaned over to look out the window. She'd had the same impression the first time she flew here.

"How far do we have to go in the car?"

"Not too far. About an hour."

Emma had always been a great traveler, but Jesse understood her impatience. She, too, was ready to be home.

"Do you think Roxy and Boomer have forgotten me?"

"No way. Roxy has been lost without you to run around with," Jesse said.

With their suitcases collected, they were finally on their way home. Once on the highway, Jesse started talking again about the town.

"There is a great diner where I like to have breakfast. And the people are really friendly. They have the best chocolate shakes around."

Emma looked out the window not saying much.

"We have a really nice neighbor, Zach. He's a horse trainer and has some really pretty horses."

"Do you think he'd let me ride them?" Emma asked. She didn't love the sport as much as Jesse, but still liked to ride for fun.

"I'm sure he will." Jesse knew Zach would like Emma. Most people did. She was friendly and outgoing, and for a seven-year-old, very intelligent. Although she loved being with kids her own age, Emma adapted easily to being around adults and most adults enjoyed her company. She wanted to learn about everything and asked questions that made most people think she was older than seven. She also insisted on helping with whatever she could.

"Here we are," Jesse said when they turned down the drive to the ranch. She let Emma unbuckle and hop in the front seat. She drove along slowly, pointing out to Emma where their property was. When a small buck darted out from behind a tree, Emma laughed with delight.

When they climbed the stairs to the house, the dogs were

jumping on the door. Once it was opened, they headed straight for Emma.

"They remember me," she said, beaming.

Jesse's heart soared at her daughter's smile. Everything would be alright.

●

Jesse was lying in bed trying to fall asleep. She knew her daughter would refuse to sleep in her own room in a new house. Jesse didn't mind. She'd missed Emma so much she didn't want the little girl too far away.

When phone rang, Jesse grabbed it before it woke Emma.

"Hey there, you made it back." Jesse smiled at the sound of Zach's voice. "I didn't wake you, did I?"

"No. Emma just fell asleep and I didn't want her to wake up," Jesse said as she got up to stand by the window.

"How is she doing? Settling in?"

"She seems fine, but—" Jesse looked back at Emma. "Paul promised to come and see her before she left my parents, and then backed out. She was pretty upset."

Zach could hear the sadness in Jesse's voice. He knew she desperately wanted Emma to like Montana and had a feeling that if she didn't, Jesse would pick up and move to wherever the little girl was happy.

"How about I come and pick you two up and take you to breakfast tomorrow?"

"That would be great. I want her to sleep in some."

"Her or you?"

"Funny. How about ten?"

"Ten it is."

Jesse climbed back in bed and smiled as she snuggled up to Emma. She finally felt truly settled into her new home now that her daughter was with her.

# Chapter Twenty-Two

Zach was smart, she gave him that.

When he arrived the next morning to pick them up, he came bearing gifts. Flowers for both her and Emma, and a stuffed horse for Emma.

Emma took the horse and flowers, said thank you, then just looked up at Zach. Jesse knew what it was. Even at seven Emma liked good-looking men and Jesse could tell by the way Emma was being so quiet that she thought Zach was cute.

*Wait until she gets a look at Hunter,* Jesse thought, *and Alex and Jeremy. Oh, God, my daughter is going to start chasing cowboys around.*

"What are you laughing at?" Zach asked.

"I was just trying to figure out who Emma will have a bigger crush on. You, Hunter, Alex or Jeremy. She'll probably pass Jeremy by because of Jen, but to her, the rest of you are fair game."

"She's only seven," he said, opening the truck door for her.

"Yeah, but she has excellent taste." She brushed against him as she got into the truck.

Emma answered any questions Zach asked about her visit to her grandparents and her plane ride. Other than that, she didn't say much. Jesse knew she'd open up soon; it never took long.

When they walked into the diner there was a huge sign that said *Welcome Emma* above the booth Jesse usually sat in. Jesse could have cried. She looked at Zach and he just shrugged as if he had nothing to do with it.

"You must be Emma," Jen said with a big smile on her face. "Your mom has been so excited about you coming. Every morning when she came in, she'd tell me how many days it would be until you got here."

"Really?" Emma asked.

"She sure did. Now, what can I get you to drink while you look over the menu?"

Emma ordered her usual chocolate milk, and Zach and Jesse ordered coffee. A few minutes later, Bill wandered in.

"Well now, it's about time you got here," Bill said to Emma, holding out his hand for her to shake.

"Emma," Jesse said, "this is Zach's grandfather, Bill." Emma took his hand and said hello.

"Now be sure to come by my store when you're done here. We have to make sure you have a proper cowgirl hat since you live on a ranch now."

Emma beamed. "Really? I can get a hat?"

"You're going to need a hat if you're going to come out and ride my pony," Zach answered.

"Really? You'll let me ride your pony?"

"Of course. Your mom said you like to ride and I have a pony that's too little for me, so I need someone small. Think you can help me out?"

Emma nodded. "Yes, yes, yes."

Zach smiled. He wasn't sure how much it would take to win Emma over, but he wanted to give it his all. He looked at her sitting next to Jesse, their heads together looking at the menu trying to decide what to eat. It was obvious Jesse was her mother, with her brown eyes and hair. Zach was sure Jesse looked exactly like Emma when she was little.

"So, what's it gonna be?" Jen asked when she same back for their order.

"Pancakes," Jesse and Emma said at the same time. This made Emma giggle. Jesse listened to her daughter laugh, her heart so filled with love. Emma was her life. She wanted her to have a home full of love and support. Jesse wanted her to have a childhood she would remember forever.

Now that Zach said she could ride, Emma bombarded him with questions about the pony.

"Is it a boy or girl?"

"A girl."

"What color is she?"

"She's brown with white legs."

"Is she tall? Mom used to let me ride Bear and he was really tall."

"She's about this high," Zach said, holding his hand up.

Jesse couldn't remember seeing a horse that looked like that at Zach's before, and she definitely knew there had been no ponies.

"What's her name?"

"Candy."

Emma thought about this, trying to decide if it was a good name or not. Deciding that it was, she asked, "Can we ride her today?"

"If your mom says it's okay."

"Mom?" Emma asked with pleading eyes.

"Of course we can go today as long as we aren't keeping you from anything, Zach."

"Nope. I cleared my day to spend it with two beautiful ladies."

Emma beamed. *He's really, really good*, Jesse thought.

After breakfast they headed to Bill's where he outfitted Emma in a "real" cowgirl outfit, complete with boots, hat and chaps.

When they pulled in front of Zach's barn, Emma jumped out and ran over to the corral. Inside was a gleaming bay pony. Emma stuck her hand out for the mare to smell.

When the pony nibbled at her hand, Emma declared, "She likes me."

Jesse watched as Zach put the halter on so Emma could lead the pony into the barn.

"When did you get this pony?" Jesse asked. "I don't remember ever seeing her here."

Zach just smiled and walked into the barn.

Jesse watched as Zach helped Emma groom and tack Candy. The pony seemed very sweet and stood patiently as Emma put the bridle on.

"Look, Mom. I can reach her head without help."

Watching Zach with Emma made Jesse's heart ache. *Zach is going to be a great dad,* she thought. Jesse pictured him with his own son or daughter, helping them, teaching them.

Emma led Candy out into the ring. Zach followed behind and Jesse stopped him. "Did you get this pony just for Emma?"

"I couldn't help it. The pony needed a home and I knew Emma would feel better if she had an immediate friend. I hope that's okay"

"Thank you."

Jesse turned away as he walked into the ring. She didn't want him to see the tears in her eyes. The fact that he'd taken time to think about her daughter, a little girl he'd never even met, was more than Jesse could take.

"Mommy. Mom, look at me." Emma sat proudly on the pony walking a circle around Zach. Emma listened to the directions Zach gave her and did her best to do as he said.

"That's probably enough for today. Once you get going, me, you and your mom can take a ride together," she heard Zach say.

"Can I come back out tomorrow?" Emma asked.

"Well." Zach glanced at Jesse. "Why don't you talk to your mom about when it's good for her to come over? You can come anytime as long as your mom is with you."

"Mom!"

Jesse knew Emma would bug her to death. "We'll talk about it tonight."

Zach drove them home and watched as Emma ran up the steps to let the dogs out. He leaned against the truck door with his arms around Jesse's waist.

"You didn't have to go to all that trouble."

"It wasn't any trouble." He leaning in for a kiss.

"You know she's going to drive me crazy about coming over there now."

"I'm counting on it." Zach smiled before kissing her again. "I'll see you tomorrow?"

"I imagine you'll see us almost every day. I hope you're ready."

"I'm ready. Good night, Emma," Zach yelled before getting into the truck.

Emma waved as she ran around with the dogs.

Emma walked over to Jesse after Zach pulled away. "You like him, Mom, don't you?"

Jesse put her arm around Emma's shoulder. "Yes, Emma. I like him a lot."

# Chapter Twenty-Three

$O$ver the next few weeks, Emma convinced Jesse to take her over to ride Candy almost every afternoon. Not that it took much convincing, because Jesse wanted to see Zach.

In the mornings they'd go over to the diner for breakfast, then go over to see Gator so Jesse could ride and do her lessons.

Emma made friends with the younger kids who were at the barn, so she enjoyed going there. She was usually exhausted by evening and fell asleep leaving Jesse to sit outside and relax.

Zach came over a few nights and they took to necking on the deck—something Jesse thought she enjoyed more than sex. Well, maybe not more than sex, but it definitely got the blood pumping.

"Zach, I'd like you to stay over, maybe this weekend."

"Are you sure?"

"Yes. Emma loves being around you and she knows I 'like' you. She's informed me more than once that she's seen us kissing."

"I'm so glad to hear you like me," Zach said, nuzzling her neck. Jesse stretched to one side giving him free access to her neck and throat.

"I'll mention it to her and see what she says. If she is totally against it, we'll wait."

"Okay by me," he said and continued to work on her neck. "But you know, a blanket under that tree over there might work for now."

Jesse looked at the tree, then back at Zach and just about ran into the house for a blanket.

"So we're all set for Friday night?" Zach asked.

"Yes. Emma said as long as you bring pizza you can come over. We're going to watch the rodeo. She wants to see who Hunter is."

Emma had talked to Hunter almost daily after she had answered the phone once when he had called. She was thoroughly impressed that he rode bulls, and he had promised to let her pet a bull next time the rodeo came through.

When Zach arrived, he noted that both Jesse and Emma were in their pajamas.

"It's a pajama party," Emma informed him. "Didn't you bring yours?" she asked.

Jesse had to laugh at the uncomfortable look Zach had on his face. How do you tell a seven-year-old you didn't wear pajamas? Jesse took pity on him and told Emma to get them some drinks.

When the rodeo came on, Zach tried to answer all Emma's questions. "Why do some bulls have big horns? What's that bump on his neck? Do they ever stop jumping around?"

Although she wore him out, Zach thoroughly enjoyed talking with Emma. He couldn't understand why her father had no interest in her. She was a pleasure to be around, except, Zach found out, when she was tired or hungry. Then there was no pleasing her. And giving her soda was a big no-no. He learned that the hard way after she asked him for a coke and then ran around like a lunatic for an hour.

"Here comes Hunter," Jesse said. When they flashed Hunter's picture Emma commented on how cute he was. Jesse shot Zach a knowing smile. Did she know her daughter or what?

Emma knew he had to stay on the bull for eight seconds to get the most points, and jumped up to cheer when the clock on the screen went past eight.

"I want to say hello to my friend Emma and tell her I'll see her soon," Hunter said when they interviewed him after his ride.

Emma was jumping up and down. "He said my name on TV."

"Did you give her coke?" Zach asked.

Jesse laughed. "Maybe a little. Besides, I have you to wear her down," she said just as Emma flung herself into Zach's lap.

When the rodeo was over, it took Jesse twenty minutes to convince Emma that she and Zach were not staying up but also going to bed. Suspicious, Emma refused to sleep in her own bed and insisted on sleeping between Zach and Jesse.

Jesse knew once Emma fell asleep she could be moved to her own bed, but poor Zach looked so uncomfortable when Emma again asked him about his pajamas.

"You really should have brought some," she told him.

Zach moved Emma to her own bed and stripped down before climbing in next to Jesse.

Jesse couldn't help but smile at him. "Didn't realize what you were in for when you agreed to this sleep-over, did you?"

"The question is," he said, covering her with his body. "Do you know what *you're* in for?"

Jesse grinned. "Surprise me."

# Chapter Twenty-Four

*J*esse looked out the window and wondered if she was doing the right thing. It was the day before Thanksgiving and Paul was coming to visit.

He'd called a week ago to say he wanted to see Emma for the holiday. Jesse could have come up with some excuse so he couldn't come. It would have been easy to convince him not to come, but she knew that would be wrong. She just prayed he'd show up and Emma wouldn't get hurt.

Things had been going perfectly. She and Zach were getting along great and Emma loved him. He continued teaching her to ride as well as how to take care of her pony. She was flourishing under the attention Zach gave her and Jesse didn't want to ruin that.

She had also settled into school. Emma was able to meet children her own age before school started. Jesse made it a point to attend church every Sunday and any functions around town so she and Emma would meet people and feel more at home.

Emma wanted to start taking dance lessons because some of her friends were, and she'd even been invited to a few sleepovers. With her birthday coming up soon and she was already making a list of friends to invite.

Jesse sighed. Maybe Paul had changed and would give Emma the attention she craved. The fact he'd called to say he'd like to visit had Jesse hoping he was finally making an effort. Jesse heard the car coming down the drive.

"Emma," she called. "Your dad's here."

Emma came running down the stairs with the biggest smile on her face. "Daddy," she said, running out the door.

Jesse followed her outside and stood on the deck. She watched as Paul scooped Emma up.

"How's my girl?" he asked as Emma hugged his neck. "Hey," he said to Jesse. He walked up the stairs and gave her a kiss on the cheek. "Nice place. Kind of in the middle of nowhere."

Jesse sighed. He was already starting. Seemed like he always followed a compliment with some type of criticism.

"That's why we like it," Jesse said, turning to walk in the house. Emma held on to Paul's hand like he would disappear if she let it go.

"It's freezing here. What is it, like fifteen degrees out?" he said with a look of distaste.

"It's Montana, Paul. I told you to bring warm clothes."

"California is the place to be. Great weather. Houses are near stuff."

"I'll take your word on that," Jesse said. "Emma, why don't you show your dad around?"

Emma grabbed Paul's hand, pulling him along. "Here's where all my toys are and …"

Jesse could hear Emma's excitement. Although she wasn't glad to see Paul herself, she was glad he came for Emma. She'd endure his comments and be pleasant for her.

She wished she could see Zach. Jesse had really wanted to spend the holiday with him and his family. Hunter had even come into town.

The Bakers were the type of family Jesse always wished to be part of. They enjoyed spending time together, had great stories to tell about growing up, and listened to each other without putting one another down when the other didn't agree.

They'd all welcomed Jesse and Emma with open arms when they joined them at the Labor Day barbecue. Like Jesse, Emma had immediately taken to Zach's mother. Amanda treated

Emma as she did her own grandchildren. Zach's niece Katie had become Emma's best friend and slept over several times. The girls were inseparable when they were together.

Zach's family made Jesse and Emma feel so at home that it was like she and Emma were truly part of the family.

Yes, the Bakers were the type of family Jesse had always wanted.

"And she has white on her legs and I can ride her alone. Mom, Dad wants to see Candy. Can we take him to see her?" Emma looked up at Jesse with pleading eyes.

Jesse looked over at Paul, who was eyeing the big screen TV in the corner. *Probably dying to watch football.* Paul hated horses and would never come within fifty feet of them when he and Jesse were together. He'd never come to see her ride and refused to let Emma learn.

"Sure. If we hurry we can get there before she gets her dinner."

"Yay!" Emma said jumping up and down. "I'll get my hat."

Emma ran off to her bedroom to get her cowgirl hat. She never rode Candy without it and had made Jesse go back home more than once when she had forgotten it.

"Do you want to borrow a heavier jacket and gloves?" Jesse asked, putting on her own scarf and heavy coat.

"No, I'm fine. We won't be too long, will we?" Paul asked, looking at the big screen again.

Jesse could have slapped him. He hadn't changed. He'd seen Emma, given her ten minutes of attention, and now it was all about what he wanted.

"Emma, don't forget your gloves," Jesse called and walked out the door.

Paul drove while Jesse gave him the brief directions to Zach's. Jesse had spoken to Emma about not mentioning Zach in front of Paul. It's not that Jesse didn't want Paul to know that she was seeing someone, it just wasn't any of his business. She preferred to let him think she was alone and crushed because they were no longer together.

"God, does it ever get warm here?" Paul said. He stuffed his hands in his pockets.

"Come on, Daddy. Wait till you see her. I can brush her and take care of her myself." Emma smiled up at her dad and Jesse's heart tightened.

"I'm sure she's great honey. Let's see her and get back to the house."

Jesse was going lose it. Would it kill him to be excited for Emma for just an hour? Emma ran ahead to Candy's stall and opened the door.

"Should she be going in there by herself?" Paul asked.

"Emma has become an excellent horse person. She's a great student and has learned a lot," Jesse said, not adding that she wasn't the one who'd been teaching Emma about horses.

Emma tied Candy and starting brushing her. "See how I can reach her head by myself, Daddy? She just stands there and lets me take care of her." The pony nuzzled Emma's hand looking for a treat. "Come pet her Daddy. She won't hurt you."

"I'm fine over here, honey. I can see you. You're doing a great job." Paul shivered. "Are you almost done?"

Jesse'd had it. "Can I talk to you outside?" she said walking away, forcing Paul to follow. She turned to face him, anger in her eyes. "What's your problem? Did you come all the way here to spend time with your daughter, or sit and watch TV?"

"I *am* spending time with her."

"Oh, yeah," Jesse said, trying not to raise her voice. "You gave her a hug, saw her room and then eyed the TV the rest of the time."

"I didn't come all the way here to listen to you preach to me about being a father, Jesse."

Jesse looked toward the barn door to be sure Emma was still inside. "Then *be* a father. Give her your attention. Be excited about the things that make her excited, even if you just pretend. That was always your problem, Paul. You never got excited for other people, but always wanted us to be excited for you."

"Why should I be excited about being in a state I never wanted to set foot in? It's freezing here and you live in the middle of nowhere. Are there even any other people around here?"

Jesse knew he wouldn't understand why she'd chosen Montana. Paul had never been an outdoors person. He preferred flash, where she preferred simple. He'd never change, and he'd never understand her or Emma.

"Can't she hurry up?"

"You need to keep your voice down."

"Why? She can't hear us out here. I saw the stupid pony, so we can leave."

Jesse looked up to see Emma standing in the barn doorway holding Candy by the bridle. Emma turned and climbed up into the saddle.

"Emma," Jesse called. But Emma just turned Candy and rode back behind the barn and up the over the hill.

"Great, now where is she going?" Paul said, throwing his hands up.

Jesse took a breath. "You need to leave now. Go back to the airport, get on a plane, and leave."

"What? What did I do?"

Jesse was yelling now, tears in her eyes. "She was so excited you were coming. All she could talk about was how she was going to show you how she could ride her pony. For once couldn't you have sucked it up and pretended to be interested in what she was doing?"

Jesse walked toward him, forcing him to back against the car. "Leave and don't plan on coming back. If Emma wants to see you again, I will bring her to you."

"You can't keep me from her," Paul yelled.

"Oh, I wouldn't dream of it. But something tells me I won't have to worry about her wanting to see you."

"She loves me, Jesse."

"Yes she does. And every time you're near her, you break

her heart," Jesse yelled. "Go, now!"

Paul just stared at her, then turned and got in the car. Jesse watched to make sure he was gone before she turned to the barn. She didn't think Emma would have gone far and may even be watching from a distance.

Going into the barn to wait, she headed for Zach's office. Sitting behind the desk, Jesse cried. She cried for her failed marriage. She cried because she didn't want to hate Paul. But mostly she cried for Emma, who once again would be heartbroken her dad had let her down.

Wiping her face, Jesse got up and walked to the barn door. She was worried—Emma should have been back by now. It had only been about a half hour, but it was cold out and would be getting dark soon. What if Emma had fallen and was hurt? She was upset when she left and probably not concentrating on riding. Jesse started to get scared. Emma could be lost. She could freeze when it got dark.

Jesse went to Ty's stall and got him out to tack him. She couldn't just sit here and wait; she had to go and look for Emma. While she got Ty ready, Jesse's fear grew as horrible visions of what could happen to Emma ran through her head.

•

The look on Jesse's tear-stained face told Zach there was something very wrong.

"What is it?" he asked. She was shaking as she tried to buckle Ty's bridle straps.

"It's Emma," Jesse choked out. "She's gone."

"Gone?"

"I have to go find her. She could be hurt. She could freeze out there," Jesse cried. "I should never have let him come." The tears flowed down Jesse's face. "Zach, we have to find her. She's all alone—"

"Get one of the other horses ready," Zach said to Alex, who was with him. Zach grabbed Jesse's shoulder and made her look up at him. "Tell me what happened."

"Paul. He upset Emma. Emma heard him say things about

us living here and about Candy just being a stupid horse. She rode off on Candy. She's been gone so long. She could be hurt. She rode off upset. She could have fallen."

Zach's jaw clenched. He already knew Emma's father was a jerk and now the little girl could be in danger because of him.

"Call Bill. Tell him to come and stay with you." He finished tightening the girth on Ty.

"What do you mean? I'm going to look for her."

Zach turned to Jesse. "You're in no condition to ride. You're upset and scared. Alex and I will find Emma. You stay here in case she comes back."

"No, I want to go with you. She's my daughter."

"And I'll find her." Zach led Ty out of the barn. Alex was already mounted and waiting for him. Zach mounted Ty. "We'll find her, Jesse. Call Bill." With that, he and Alex rode off.

Jesse just stood there wringing her hands and staring after them. She couldn't stop the tears. The thought of something happening to Emma was ripping her apart. "Dear God, please let my baby be alright." Jesse went into the house to call Bill.

Zach's anger at Jesse's ex was replaced by concern for Emma, at least for now. Emma had become a good rider. Zach had taken both her and Jesse out on several rides to teach them how to find their way home, as well as what to do if they ever got hurt while riding alone. One of the main things was to always tell someone where you were headed, but of course Emma didn't do that this time.

He knew Emma was sensitive about her father. She had never really mentioned him to Zach, and Zach had never asked. According to Jesse, Emma worshipped her dad even though he always seemed to let her down.

Zach headed east hoping Emma would have gone in the direction he'd ridden with her in the past. He loved going out with her and Jesse. Everything was so new to them that they had him looking at the land in a new way. He smiled, remembering how Jesse and Emma had made him look at the rock formations and try to figure out what animals they looked like.

The elephant Emma had swore was there looked more like a bug that had been squished by an elephant to Zach. Zach was hoping it was that elephant Emma had headed for.

Emma always wanted to come back to those rocks because she liked to climb up and look down at the surrounding area. She said she felt like she was on top of the world up there.

As Zach rode closer to the elephant rocks, relief flooded him. Candy was grazing peacefully beside the rocks and he looked up to see someone sitting on top. He and Alex rode up slowly as not to startle Emma.

"Well hey there," he said, smiling. "What's a pretty girl like you doing way out here?"

Emma didn't move. She was sitting up with her knees to her chest and arms wrapped around. Her head was buried in between. Zach could see her shaking, but he wasn't sure if it was from crying or being cold.

Zach got off Ty and turned to Alex. "Ride back and tell Jesse we found her. She seems okay. I'll be behind you shortly."

Alex nodded and rode off.

Zach climbed the rocks and sat next to Emma, placing a blanket over her shoulders. "I sure do love it up here. You can see everything around you."

He waited, hoping Emma would say something. He wanted to take her and hug her and tell her everything would be okay.

"Emma," he said softly. "Your mom told me what happened." Zach heard sniffling and went on. "I'm sure your dad didn't mean what he said. Your mom says—"

Emma raised her head. "He did mean it. He called Candy stupid. He's the stupid one," she cried.

Zach looked into her puffy red eyes. What could he say when he agreed with her?

"He never likes anything I like. All he cares about are his stupid friends, and stupid football."

Zach handed her a rag from his pocket so she could wipe her face. Emma cried harder. "Why can't he love me?"

Zach heart broke. He put his arm around Emma and pulled her to his side. "Emma, sometimes it's hard for dads to understand their little girls. Just because he doesn't like the things you like doesn't mean he doesn't love you."

Zach wanted to tell Emma what a loser her dad was, but he didn't think that was what the seven-year-old needed to hear. "He came all the way here to see you, didn't he?"

"Yeah, but then he said all those mean things. I heard him arguing with mommy. He doesn't care about us. Why can't he be like you?" Emma asked, looking up at Zach. "You always help me and never yell at me or call my ideas stupid."

Zach looked down at the little girl he'd come to love and wasn't sure what to say. "Emma, you and I are lucky because we like a lot of the same things. That's what makes us such great friends. But there are things you like to do that I don't."

Emma looked up at him and sniffled. "Like what?"

"Well." Zach didn't want to hurt her feeling more. "I hate to tell you, but ..." Zach bent lower so he was whispering. "I really don't like playing Barbies. If anyone found out, they'd make fun of me."

"But you play Barbies with me all the time," Emma said like she couldn't believe what she was hearing.

"That's because I don't want to hurt your feelings. I think your dad is just not sure how to tell you he doesn't like doing some things. So instead he always tells you he's busy or he can't. It's just his way."

Zach could see Emma shivering under the blanket. He looked up and knew it would be dark soon, which meant it would get a lot colder.

"Emma, your mom is really worried about you. Why don't we ride back to the house? Candy needs her dinner. We can make some hot chocolate and watch whatever movie you want."

"What about my dad?"

"Your dad is gone. Your mom sent him home."

Emma dried her face. "Hot chocolate sounds good."

Zach stood up and helped Emma climb down the rocks. He took Candy's reins and looped them around his saddle. "Why don't you ride up here with me so you can start warming up?" He settled Emma in front of him and wrapped the blanket around her then headed for home.

•

Jesse was frantic by the time Bill arrived. She was walking into the barn to saddle another horse when he pulled up. "Come in the house. Let's make some coffee. They'll need it when they get back," he said.

While Bill made coffee she told him what happened. "She just rode off. I could tell she was upset." When Bill placed a mug in front of her, Jesse looked up at him. "If anything happens to her—"

"Nothing is going to happen to her. Zach will find her and bring her home." Bill filled their mugs for a second time while he listened to Jesse talk about her ex-husband.

"He wasn't a bad man in the sense you think a man is bad. He just was not attentive. He always thought of himself first. I always put Emma before myself and him, and I think he was jealous of that."

"Some men just aren't meant to be dads," Bill said.

Jesse gave him a small smile. She could see the concern on Bill's face and was glad Zach had her call him; it helped to have him there while she waited.

Both she and Bill jumped up when they heard the hoof beats. Jesse ran out the door and onto the porch just as Alex came to a stop.

"We found her. She's fine. Zach's bringing her back."

Bill came up and put his arms around Jesse as she started to cry all over again.

"Put Star away. We have coffee inside," Bill told him. Alex nodded and headed for the barn.

Jesse hugged Bill. "He found her. He found my baby."

"Let's get some fresh coffee on and some food together. I'm sure Emma will be hungry when she gets here."

Jesse tried to help Bill but she couldn't stop looking out the window. Finally, she saw them coming down the hill. Candy was tied to Ty's saddle and Emma sat in front of Zach with his arms wrapped tightly around her. Jesse ran out the door and met them half way across the yard.

"Mommy," Emma said.

Alex came over, took Emma from Zach, and carried her into the house.

"Put her in front of the fire so she can warm up," Bill said.

Jesse followed and immediately took Emma in her arms when Alex put her down. Holding onto Emma, Jesse cried.

"I'm sorry I ran away. Please don't be mad at me."

Jesse put her hands on Emma's face, wiping the tears away. "Emma, I'm not mad at you. I'm just glad you're home."

Zach came in and looked over at Jesse and Emma. Jesse was sitting on the floor with her back against the couch, and Emma was on her lap snuggled against her. Bill came over and handed him a steaming cup of coffee.

"Thanks," he said.

"She gonna be okay?" Bill asked.

"Yeah. She was just upset and cold when we found her."

Bill looked at his grandson. "How did you know where to find her?"

Zach set his cup down and looked at him. "Because I listen to Emma." Zach walked over and squatted down. "How about that hot chocolate?"

Emma nodded her head and snuggling back into Jesse.

Jesse looked at Zach, "Thank you. Thank you for bringing her home."

Zach smiled and reached out to wipe the tears from Jesse's face. "You're welcome."

Bill and Alex put their coats on to leave. "I'll drop Alex off on my way home. You all set here?"

Zach looked at Jesse and Emma. "Yeah, I think we're good

for now." Zach ran his hands through his hair and over his face.

"You okay?" Bill asked.

"Yeah," he said shaking his head. "Emma could have—"

"But she didn't and she's home," Bill said cutting him off.

Zach came and sat by Jesse. He handed a warm cup of hot chocolate to Emma. "Extra chocolaty."

He looked at Jesse. "Do you want me to take you home?"

Jesse looked down at Emma who was still in her lap. "Emma?" She pushed the hair from Emma's eyes. "Are you ready to go home?"

Emma shook her head. "I want to stay here with Zach."

Jesse looked at Zach.

"How about that movie? I said you could pick it," he said to Emma.

Jesse looked at Zach with all the emotions she felt inside. Never before had she been so scared. Jesse knew how much he loved her and Emma. He said so with every one of his actions.

"I should run home and check on the dogs," Jesse said.

Zach stood. "I have a better idea. How about I run to town and pick up a pizza and the dogs. While I'm gone, you two can pick out the movie."

Jesse smiled. "That sounds perfect. How about it, Emma? Should we make Zach watch a girlie movie tonight?"

Emma giggled.

Zach bent and gave them each a kiss on the head. "I'll be back."

Emma looked up at Jesse. "I didn't mean to run off. Daddy just made me so mad when he called Candy stupid."

Jesse watched as tears welled in Emma's eyes and tried not to cry. There was nothing worse than seeing your child hurting.

"I went and sat on the elephant rock and cried. I was just going to sit there for a little bit. Then I started to get cold and I didn't want to move," Emma said sniffling. "But I didn't get scared. I knew Zach would come and get me."

Jesse didn't know what to say. Zach made her feel the same way. So she just held Emma and thanked God Zach had come into their lives.

# Chapter Twenty Five

"Mommy is this the last present to wrap?"

"That's it. We're all finished."

"Do you think Zach will like his gifts?"

"I think he will." Jesse sat back on her heels and looked at the pile of gifts under the Christmas tree. Then, she stood and took Emma to bed.

Jesse was excited about Christmas. She and Zach had grown a lot closer since Thanksgiving. He'd become very protective of Emma and was spending most evenings with them. Both Jesse and Emma had put that awful day behind them, but Jesse felt better knowing Zach always took extra care to make sure he knew where Emma was.

Jesse wanted the first Christmas in their new home to be perfect. They'd decided to just spend Christmas Eve with the three of them together at her home, and tomorrow they'd spend the day with Zach's family.

After the holidays, work on the new barn would pick up and be completed in a few months. Although Jesse would take boarders immediately, she decided to wait until the spring to start the therapy riding program. She'd have an easier time recruiting people when the weather was warmer. It would also allow her time to find proper staff and give them some time to work together before having clients. She was hoping she could convince Jen to take on the job of barn manager. It would give Jen evenings free to start taking the business classes she talked about.

"She asleep?" Zach asked as he walked into the room.

"Just about. She promised me she'd stay in bed."

Jesse sat down next to Zach in front of the fire. "I think Christmas Eve is the only night she actually stays in bed for fear of not getting presents from Santa."

"Speaking of presents," Zach said, holding his hand out between them.

"But it's not Christmas yet." She looked down at the small box in his hand.

"It doesn't have to be Christmas for me to give this to you," Zach said as he opened the box.

Jesse's breath caught. Inside was a beautiful diamond and sapphire ring. But what made this ring so unique was that it was two horseshoes linked together.

Zach put his hand under Jesse's chin, lifting her face. Jesse could see the love in his eyes. "I love you Jesse, more than I ever thought possible. You and Emma make my life complete. I want to be all the things you've ever wanted. Marry me, Jesse."

Tears welled in Jesse's eyes. Just months before, her life was in shambles, and her dreams seemed so far away. Yet sitting in front of her was a man who loved her and her daughter, a man she knew she could trust and rely on—a man she knew would always be there for her.

"I love you, Zach. More than I ever thought it was possible to love someone. You are my heart and soul. You are the part of me that was always missing. I couldn't live my life without you."

Jesse looked at the ring and back at Zach. With tears in her eyes, all she could do was nod her head yes.

When he slipped the ring on her finger the feeling that settled over her was one she had never felt. She loved and was loved.

"I have one more gift for you," he said, leaning toward her.

Jesse's body tingled in anticipation of what she knew was coming. "But you've given me so much already."

"Well, if you'd rather not have it?" Zach asked, and moved away from her.

Grabbing the front of his shirt she pulled him onto her as she let herself fall back.

Jesse wrapped her arms around his neck. "I didn't say that, it's just—" Zach kissed her neck and she had trouble remembering what she was going to say. "If you keep giving me all these wonderful presents—" Jesse gave a soft moan as he nibbled on her ear. "You'll have to work hard to top the previous one."

"I think this next one will definitely top the last."

•

Zach was having visions of sugar plums when he heard Emma.

"Mommy, Zach, get up! Santa came." Emma came barreling in the bedroom and leapt onto the bed.

"Welcome to Christmas morning with a seven-year-old," Jess said.

Zach sat up and was glad he'd put on the pajamas Emma had given him as an early gift. She insisted he open them last night so he'd have something to wear to bed. Zach watched as Jesse tried to wash her face while Emma stood in the bathroom door trying to hurry her along.

"Come on, Mom. You look fine," Emma said, bouncing up and down.

"Alright, I'm coming." Jesse stopped to kiss Zach on her way out the door. Her lips were pulled from his because Emma was pulling her through the door.

"Oh my, Emma, I guess Santa found our new home," Jesse said, smiling at Emma.

Although she tried to limit what she bought at Christmas, Jesse couldn't help herself this year.

"Hold on. Zach will be right down." She laughed as Emma vigorously shook gifts.

"Zach, look!" Emma yelled as he came down the stairs.

"Wow, you must have been an awfully good girl this year."

Zach watched Emma rip paper off the first gift. "Are you sure some of those aren't for me and your mom?" he asked.

"No," Emma replied tearing into another gift. "Santa only brings stuff for kids."

Zach sipped his coffee and watched Jesse help Emma open her gifts, oohing and aahing at everything. It was amazing how Jesse could act so surprised after having bought all the gifts.

Emma beamed up at Jesse. "Santa knows just what I like," she said, holding up a pair of new cowboy boots.

Ripping through the last few packages, Emma stopped. "Mom." She held the small box out. "This one has your name on it."

Jesse took the box and looked at the tag. "To Jesse, Love Santa," she read.

Trying to hide a smile, she glanced over at Zach who just shrugged.

"Open it, Mom."

Jesse unwrapped the paper to find a wooden box with running horses carved on it. She ran he fingers over the design.

"Is there anything in it?" Emma asked.

Jesse lifted the cover to find a piece of paper inside. "Dear Jesse," she read out loud. "I've been watching you this year and have seen how hard you've been working. I've left you a very special gift in the barn. It was too big to get in the house, but I knew it would be safe outside."

Emma jumped up. "Come on, Mom. We have to go see what it is." Emma ran over to the door and grabbed her jacket.

"Hold on. It's freezing outside. Put your boots on and don't forget your gloves."

Emma made an exasperated face, but did as she was told.

Once Jesse and Zach were also bundled up, the three of them set out toward the barn.

"What do you think it is?" Emma asked with excitement in her voice.

"I don't know. Maybe it's a new car?"

"Why would Santa leave a car in the barn?"

"Maybe because it would have been covered with snow by morning and your mom would never have found it," Zach said laughing.

Emma broke away from them and ran toward the barn, but stopped at the door to wait for them. Zach opened the door and let Jesse and Emma go in first.

"I don't see anything, Mom. Maybe Santa left your gift in Zach's barn."

Emma turned around to face Jesse, but before Jesse could look down at her to reply, she caught movement out of the corner of her eye. When Jesse raised her head, her breath caught as she raised her hand to her mouth. A giant grey head had emerged from a stall at the end of the row.

"Mom, look!" Emma ran down the aisle to the stall. She stopped and reached out her hand. "Hey, he looks just like Bear."

By now tears ran down Jesse's face. She slowly walked to the stall not believing what she saw. When she came to stop in front of the stall, she raised her hand to stroke the grey neck she'd missed so much.

"That's because it *is* Bear."

As she stroked the side of his face, he raised his nose to Jesse's face and breathed in her scent. Still not believing the horse she'd loved with all her heart was standing in front of her, Jesse turned to look at Zach.

Zach had stayed back and just watched Jesse with the horse. They'd been apart for months, but Zach knew the horse recognized Jesse. He'd stuck his head out of the stall and given a soft whinny when he heard her voice.

Zach patted Bear on the neck.

"How?" Jesse asked, wiping the tears from her face.

Zach smiled. "I want you to have everything you've ever wanted."

Sniffling, Jesse turned back to Bear.

"Are you going to ride him today, Mom?"

"No, not today. I think he might need a day or so to get used to his new home."

"Emma, let's go inside and start breakfast," Zach said scooping up Emma. "I say pancakes."

Jesse listened to them discussing the breakfast menu as they walked away. She was getting cold, but was afraid if she left Bear in the barn alone he'd disappear. Opening the stall door, she stepped in.

The giant horse immediately nuzzled her. "Sorry, boy," she said stroking his neck. "If I'd known you were out here, I would have brought some treats. I promise to bring some out later."

Jesse leaned up against Bear and put her arms around his huge neck. She stepped back and gave him one last pat and walked out of the stall.

When she got to the barn door, she stopped and looked out at her home. The kitchen light was on and she could see Zach and Emma through the windows.

Other than for Emma, Jesse had never felt more love for anyone than she did for Zach. The light caught the glittering ring on her hand. Zach was her soul mate.

In only a short time, he'd come to know her better than anyone. He anticipated her wants and needs. He shared her hopes and dreams, and he made her feel as no man ever had.

Jesse looked down at the ring one more time, then over her shoulder to the horse that was watching her.

When she turned her attention back to the house, she saw Zach looking out the window at her. Jesse smiled and walked toward her home, her daughter, and the man she loved.

● ● ●

# Maggie Grey

*Born and raised in Rhode Island, Maggie is the youngest of five children. A writer and therapeutic riding instructor, she says the only sport she was "remotely good at" was horseback riding! She currently resides in Georgia with her husband and daughter.*